Chronicles of Twierks

Sci-Fi Adventure Series

Book 5

I0631714

DRAGONS DO NOT WRITE MEMOIRS

A Novel

Tetyana Butler

Also by Tetyana Butler

Adventures of the Little Adoleeseet
Chronicles of Twierks, Book 1

The Secrets of Daeya
Chronicles of Twierks, Book 2

Treasures of the Jeweler
Chronicles of Twierks, Book 3

Quantum Witches
Chronicles of Twierks, Book 4

For more information on the books from series Chronicles of Twierks visit http://www.Twierks.com

ISBN: 978-1-948503-08-2

Printed in the United States of America

Acknowledgements

Special thanks to Nataliya Nechukhaeva for her involvement in testing all the twists and adventures that befell the heroes of the book.

And, of course, I express my enormous gratitude to the great master Brian Kaufman for editing the manuscript.

Contents

Chapter 0. The Very Beginning. Or not the very. Or not the beginning.

Location: Unknown
Time: Undetermined

Our old acquaintances Adamant and Ecktoral have settled into comfortable chairs in the mysterious room without doors or windows. This is a problem. There is no entrance. There is no exit.

How did they get inside? It's a mystery.

"Today I'll show you the adventures of Davkaleon after he got the jeweler Piromis' notes," Ecktoral said. He nodded his head, and one of the walls transformed into a screen.

"Okay," Adamant agreed, "and don't forget to show me Heather."

They speak of two young people (Davkaleon and Heather) who you know from previous adventures. Don't you know them? No matter. You'll learn everything soon enough...

Chapter 1. Manuscripts of the jeweler Piromis

Country: Daeya

Time: Long, Long Ago

Davkaleon's brother Elfid entered the room carrying a stack of papers, a confused expression on his face. "I've brought you copies of the first three manuscripts of the jeweler," he said. "The third manuscript bears the image of the sign mentioned in the jeweler's note. However, I don't know how this will help you. The sign supposedly leads to *Attl*. I've never heard about Attl, and I don't think it is in Daeya. The manuscripts do not tell exactly where this unknown Attl is located or how to get there."

That was interesting! After all the effort he'd spent obtaining the notes of the jeweler, Davkaleon was curious about what was written in these manuscripts. It seemed that everyone in Daeya was hunting them. Elfid handed Davkaleon three manuscripts.

"Let's go to the *Mug and the Sword*," suggested Davkaleon. "My treat."

Elfid happily agreed. After dinner, Davkaleon returned to his room and opened the first manuscript.

The First Manuscript

These are the records of the jeweler Piromis, the son of the jeweler Piromis, carved into the cliff rock, where he was transferred by the powerful magician of the Temple and resided for seven long years,

*making jewels by the order of the powerful
magician who filled them by his magical
powers.*

Davkaleon laid back on his bed, immersed in his
reading. The first manuscript was interesting, but its
content had absolutely no explanation why everyone in
Daeya had the desire to acquire the notes of the jeweler
Piromis.

The jeweler described the dwelling of the mage.
According to the mage's words, the building was under the
mighty Attl-at. As stated in the description, Attl-at was an
ocean. Davkaleon had trouble imagining how that could
be.

"What does it mean?" Davkaleon whispered. "That the
mage's dwelling was located in an underwater cave? Why
no? Who could prevent him from settling in an underwater
cave if he liked it?" Davkaleon waved his hand and
continued reading.

According to the manuscript, the *Eye of the Gods* was
right inside the dwelling, and the Mage could watch
everything he wanted on the screen. The Eye of the Gods
revealed the past and the future to the mage. The mage
taught Piromis to communicate with the Eye of the Gods,
and the jeweler could see what was happening in his
native Attl, as well as showing things both real and
invented, those that had already happened, and even
those things that had not happened yet!

The Mage knew how to control the weather, and he
taught Piromis how to do it. There were many robots in
the mage's dwelling which performed different jobs.

Davkaleon didn't know what the word 'robot' meant, but he knew from the description that it was a kind of an artificial servant. One robot cleaned, one washed, one cooked food. The Mage handed Piromis a stack of magic spells.

"You'll often be left alone; you have to be able to deal with my robots," said the Mage to Piromis.

And Piromis learned to do it. He never had to clean or wash himself. He didn't even need to cook. You sit in a comfortable chair, ask the Eye of the Gods to entertain you with something interesting and order a little robot to bring you, let's say, fried quail or baked fish. That's all! The little robot will immediately deliver everything to you. A table on wheels will drive up to you with everything you wish.

"Amazing," Davkaleon whispered. "You don't need to be born a Mage to do all this. It's enough to learn magic spells and order robots around. I wonder where I can buy one?" He'd been in magic shops, and hadn't seen one.

The Second Manuscript

During the seven years spent with the mage, the jeweler made several dozen pieces of jewelry. Of course, not Piromis but the Mage turned them into magic amulets, but everything took place in front of the jeweler's eyes.

The manuscript said that the jeweler described each

piece of jewelry he made. The Mage placed the Piromis's scrolls in Bible-at-Attl and said that the path to them could be described by the following signs:

Davkaleon recognized the symbols from the note in the Pillantelli Cave. True, there were more symbols in the note. Maybe the first few symbols showed how to get to the mysterious Attl?

"Now I have to find all the jeweler's manuscripts and then find the treasures themselves," Davkaleon thought. "If both the goblin and the salesman of magical items were willing to pay tens of thousands of sekels for a tiny note, then how much were they going to get for the witch trinkets themselves?" It was an interesting idea, but how to find that unknown Attl?

In the same manuscript, the jeweler explained the first magic amulet he'd created in the mage's dwelling. The amulet was made of a perfect emerald. Piromis said that he had never seen such a stone, although he was used to dealing with emeralds worthy of the gods. The Mage took the splendid emerald from a box, saying, "This stone is destined to play a fateful role in Attl. Not surprising, since the stone will be called the *Destiny Stone*. After you've polished the emerald, I'll cast a spell on a stone, and you'll watch the emerald turn into the most powerful amulet."

The Mage told Piromis that while the Destiny Stone was in Attl, no enemy would be able to conquer the country. If wars did occur, enemies would be defeated in the very first battle. When Piromis asked if the stone would protect its owner, the Mage answered:

"Oh yes. The one who'll keep the stone will become a real darling of fortune. He won't need doctors or guards. Enemy arrows will fly by, enemy swords will break, and enemy ambushes will be destroyed by lightning."

After reading the second manuscript, Davkaleon understood why there were so many people in Daeya who wanted to get the jeweler Piromis' notes. Who wouldn't want to have the Destiny Stone at his disposal?

The Third Manuscript

The third manuscript featured the story of an amulet called the Black Rose. Before describing the amulet, Piromis related the fascinating background to its creation. It seems that from the mage's dwelling, it was possible to get into the Dragon corridor. Piromis once found himself very close to this corridor, which left Piromis a little frightened.

On another occasion, the Mage was visited by another mage. Piromis wondered if the guest was not just a mage, but God himself! When the Mage and his guest left the dwelling, they entered a passage that suddenly appeared in the wall. Piromis followed them. The jeweler did not explain why he did it.

Davkaleon thought, *Maybe he wanted to find out if the*

mighty Attl-at flows really above him, as the Mage said? I would definitely want to check.

> *The narrow corridor led Piromis to the entrance of a cave. Piromis took another step and found himself inside the cave. At the same instant, the cave was filled with water. The floor disappeared. Water was everywhere. Piromis rushed back, realizing with horror that water would pour into the Mage's home. He had enough breath for a couple of minutes, but the corridor finished in a dead end. The entrance to the Mage's home had disappeared!*
>
> *"I wanted to see where I am," Piromis later explained to the Mage.*
>
> *"You are under the waters of Attl-at," the Mage replied. "If you dive down in the cave, find the Dragon corridor and swim along it, you will find yourself in the waters of Tartar."*

"In the waters of Tartar?" Davkaleon was surprised. "Almost like in Daeya."

In Daeya, there was Tartrar, not Tartar, but the names differed by only one letter.

> *"The waters of Tartar are very fast," the Mage explained. "They are dangerous even for those who have devoted their whole life to training and swimming in them. Tartar is*

7

remarkable because from it you can get to many unusual places. The easiest way is to get from it to the Cliff Rock. Everyone in Attl knows this place."

"Get to the Cliff Rock?" Davkaleon whispered. He was even more surprised. The Tartrar and Cliff Rock were both found in Daeya! Was the Mage's dwelling under the Cliff Rock in Daeya? Where then was Attl found? Perhaps in the past, Daeya was called Attl? It was possible, though unlikely.

Davkaleon's parents were from the old Daeyan tradition. They even forced their son to attend the old school of Daeya. In this school, students were drilled in the ancient history of Daeya, and there was not a word about *Attl*. Davkaleon read the manuscript again. What did the Mage tell the jeweler about Tartar?

The waters of Tartrar are very fast. They are dangerous even for those who have devoted their entire lives to training and swimming in them.

Davkaleon knew this. He took lessons from Master Gandall, the best trainer in Daeya, and he could dive to the distant ocean floor next to the Cliff Rock. Tartrar was rushing at its bottom, so Davkaleon was well acquainted with its waters. In Daeya, the underwater waterfall was *also* called Tartrar.

The place where the waterfall started depended on the

8

time of the day. During the highest tide, the waves rolled over the Cliff Rock, and the waterfall started about 50 meters from the rock surface. During the lowest tide, the waves barely reached the middle of the cliff. Thick splashes hung over them like white foam. It seemed that a silvery-white mist enveloped the rock.

It happened that the vortices gathered in one place and swirled, and a funnel formed at this place. Faster and faster the white foam swirled around the funnel, the whirlwinds rose higher and higher and then flew down at a frantic speed. The black emptiness was in the middle, and the waterfall of Tartrar ran down around it. The chances of surviving in this waterfall were not very high. But athletes linked victory in competitions with jumping into the Tartrar Falls!

Davkaleon, even without the jeweler's manuscripts, was going to measure his strength with this waterfall. Now he wanted to do it as quickly as possible.

"I'll have to agree tomorrow with Gandall about training in the waterfall," Davkaleon decided.

The jeweler's manuscript said, "The Tartar flows at the bottom of Attl-at. It is necessary to climb up to the Cliff Rock by 20 sazhens. There are several more ways to get there from the water cave. But they are much more dangerous than the Dragon Corridor. The Dragon Corridor can only be seen by those who have mage's blood coursing through their veins. One exception—the Dragon Corridor will be open to a one who will own the Dragon's Amulet. It was me who cut and polished the stone for this amulet, and Mage cast a spell on it and performed a ritual."

The manuscript continued. "That amulet will also be called the Black Rose or the Dragon Rose. With its help, it will be possible to get into the Dragon Corridor, provided that you are in Mage's cave or in the Chamber of the Mages or in the waters of Tartar."

The Dragon Corridor was so named because from it, you can get into Dragon-net, the dwelling of the Dragon. However, that is not the only destination. You can travel to many places, including to the dwelling of the gods and to Twierks as well.

"Twierks?!!" Davkaleon jumped as if stung. "Can one get to Twierks from the Dragon corridor?" If so, then he wouldn't need the Temple in the Rock either. It wouldn't matter if the temple threw him out for a year. He would get to Twierks in a different way!

"Wait, stop!" He would have to find the Dragon Corridor first. What did the jeweler say about this corridor? That one can get from it into the Dragon's dwelling? And the Mage called this place *Dragon-net*.

The little Adoleeseet, Chapa, told Davkaleon about the Dragon-net when he talked about the DRAGON of Adolees. He'd said, "No one dares to bother the Great DRAGON of Adolees in his Dragon-net. And not only there!"

"What if the Dragon corridor is the corridor of the DRAGON of Adolees?" Davkaleon thought. The Mage had told the jeweler about that corridor. The Mage hadn't said that the word DRAGON should be written in capital letters. That's why the jeweler wrote *Dragon corridor*. Anyone would. "I must talk to Adoleeseet Chapa-Chapius,"

Davkaleon decided.

The manuscript ended with the Piromis explanation: "I described every piece of jewelry I made. The Mage said that the way to them can be described with the help of such a drawing."

512   4913   5832

Davkaleon recognized drawings and numbers from the note from the Pillantelli Cave.

"I'll try to dive into this waterfall," thought Davkaleon. "If one can get to Tartrar from the Dragon Corridor, why can't he do the opposite? The Temple in the Rock refused to let me into Twierks? Ha! I'll find another way! First, I will get from Tartrar to the Dragon Corridor, and from there to Twierks. And there I'll attend Sciencia of the Mages and investigate the *Tender Monster*. I must find out what the *aira* is. And then finding Heather in Llill of Twierks will be as easy as shelling pears."

Heather was the girl he'd seen in the Temple, and he was anxious to see her again.

"The manuscript said that if you do not have the blood of Mages in your veins, then you will not see the Dragon Corridor. If the temple in the rock first opened the entrance for him, and then allowed him to enter the depository, then why wouldn't the Dragon Corridor do the same?"

11

Davkaleon looked at the third manuscript again. His attention was drawn to the lower end of the manuscript. It felt like a piece was torn from the papyrus. Perhaps, the papyrus was like that from the very beginning. Or perhaps not.

Chapter 2. Jumping to the Tartrar and Meeting with Heather

"Are you sure you want to test the underwater waterfall?" Gandall the trainer asked.

"Of course!" Davkaleon answered without hesitation.

"Why?"

Davkaleon did not want to answer this question. He had not told anyone except his brothers about the secret notes of the jeweler Piromis. It was better not to mention magical treasures. It was forbidden even to talk about Twierks in Daeya. Davkaleon was not going to tell anyone about his meeting with Heather in the temple and his desire to see her again. What was left to talk about? The Daeyan Jumping Competition from the Cliff Rock, of course! Especially when talking to a trainer.

"Did anyone manage to win the competition without jumping into the waterfall Tartrar?" Davkaleon asked.

"Never," the trainer answered.

"Then let's start training!"

"Not so fast," Gandall protested. "Since those who jump into the underwater waterfall have little chance of survival, I need a signed wavier that you were fully informed of the dangers and insisted on training. I have no need for lawsuits, should you move on to the afterlife."

"What do I have to sign?" asked Davkaleon impatiently.

"Listen to this before signing. As you know, the annual Rock Jumping Competition is held in Daeya. But only a few survive. About once every five years, a lucky one manages to overcome all obstacles and receives a reward.

Eternal glory surrounds the winner. As a prize, he receives the golden rose of Daeya, and his name is chiseled into the Walk of Fame in gold letters. Sounds great, right? Listen further. The competition is usually attended by as many as twenty people. Half of them survive. Disappointing statistics." He nodded his head wisely.

"But that's not all. To be admitted to the competition, it is necessary to pass qualifying tests. Do you know how many die during those tests? *Nobody ever talks about that.* I know how many of *my* students died, but I'm not the only trainer. No one requires such statistics from coaches. And even the coach might not remember how many died during training. If you still want to practice, you are welcome. All that is required of you is to sign an agreement on non-disclosure of my teaching methods and to not reveal the secrets of the Tartrar's currents." Trainer Gandall handed over the wavier and other forms.

Secrets of the Tartrar's currents? That sounded great! Davkaleon came for this.

"This is a map of the currents with explanations of what each symbol means. Until you memorize everything that is written here, do not show up in my class."

Gandall didn't have to encourage him. Davkaleon longed to remember everything related to the Tartrar.

Weeks passed in intense exercises. Gandall had an excellent simulator that repeated the Tartrar's currents. The simulator, however, was many times shorter than the real waterfall and it was easier to train on it. Still, the simulator made it possible to deal with the dangerous habits of the currents. A few weeks later, Davkaleon managed to reach the bottom of the real Tartrar.

"Now I need to figure out how to get from the Tartrar to the Dragon Corridor," he thought. Alas, no matter how hard Davkaleon tried, he failed. The current raced like crazy! At that speed, one could only leave the Dragon Corridor and not enter it.

Davkaleon continued his attempts to enter the Dragon Corridor. Some currents had names. One of them was the Fountain of Dreams. Rushing down in the Tartrar's waterfall, Davkaleon had time to think about how he dreamt of getting into the Dragon Corridor. Dreaming did not help.

Jumping into the waterfall the next time, Davkaleon imagined that he would meet Heather. Alas, this desire was not fulfilled either. After many jumps and thoughts, Davkaleon returned home. On the way, he got the idea that he'd entered the temple of Twierks' Mages with the help of the Mages' drink. Maybe, to get to the Dragon Corridor, he would also need to drink this beverage? But to prepare a Mages' potion he needed to add all the attributes that he used when he had got to the temple of Twierks—including the adamant dagger and a Mage's mask.

"The Dragon Corridor is a dangerous place; it is necessary to stock up on weapons," thought Davkaleon, preparing the Mages' potion. "One adamant dagger is not enough."

Flying in the waterfall past the Fountain of Dreams, Davkaleon had time to think about Heather. At the same instant, Davkaleon began to spin. A black haze enveloped everything around him. Some unknown power threw him to the ground, and he went rolling through the grass. The darkness began to dissipate. A monster appeared from the thickets, so ugly and huge that Davkaleon could not believe his eyes.

He jumped up, and grabbing a knife, threw it into the monster's eye. Another knife flew into the second eye. The beast roared. Davkaleon drew his sword and, running closer, jumped onto the back of the monster. The monster turned around, and Davkaleon saw Heather. His heart fluttered!

"Heather, don't worry, I'll whack this beast!" shouted Davkaleon. "For me it's a trifle!"

"Alfreydon!" the girl's voice rang joyfully. "Oh, ISIDA, thank you for your help! But this hero could perish! Look what a huge beast it is! ISIDA, please get us out of here!"

At that moment, another beast appeared.

"Heather, don't ask the goddess to take you away," Davkaleon-Alfreydon shouted. (Alfreydon was the only name she knew him by.) "I can cope with two monsters! For me, it's no big deal! I can cope with ten! And then we'll talk. I was looking for you for so long!"

Despite his plea, a sudden tornado whisked Heather away. As for Davkaleon, there were monsters to fend off.

Someone tried to pull Davkaleon off the back of the monster. Davkaleon struck him with his sword. At the same moment, the tornado spun Davkaleon and threw him onto a lawn not far from the Cliff Rock in Daeya.

"Oh, the Fountain of Dreams, what did you do to me?" Davkaleon was outraged. "Couldn't you make our meeting last longer? The fact that you threw the monster at me is good! Heather saw that I'm not a wuss! But I didn't even have time to talk to her!"

The fountain did not answer.

"It's good that she remembers Alfreydon," thought Davkaleon. "But how can I explain to her that I'm me if she saw me only in a mask and knows me as Alfreydon?"

For several days, Davkaleon persistently hopped into the Tartrar and tried to find the entrance to the Dragon Corridor or to meet Heather, but the Fountain of Dreams no longer paid attention to his wishes.

Davkaleon headed home. There his friend Chapa-Chapius from Adolees was waiting for him.

Chapter 3. Chamber of Neophytes

"You asked me about the Dragon Corridor," Chapius chattered. "I spent several weeks almost non-stop in the Adolees depository of knowledge. So that's, indeed, the DRAGON Corridor! Not of some unknown Dragon. The great DRAGON of Adolees! The place you really must get into is the Chamber of Mages! That's why I'm here. So, listen, and then we'll head there together."

It was unnecessary to ask Davkaleon to listen. He was all ears already.

"I do not know how to get to the Chamber of Mages, and where it is, but I know that before getting into the Chamber of Mages, you need to get into the Chamber of Neophyte which is located in Cliff Rock." Chapius seemed happy to explain, but then became sad and added, "on the whole, I understood it like that."

"In the Cliff Rock?" Davkaleon was delighted. "How do I get in there?"

"Actually, I'm not sure, but in the Adolees depository, it was partly explained how to do this, so we should try," Chapius said cheerfully.

There was not a word about the Chamber of Neophytes in the jeweler's manuscript, but Davkaleon had to start somewhere. He didn't mind.

"Well, tell me what you know," Davkaleon waved his hand.

Chapius told him that there were several caves in the Cliff Rock. One of them was located at the very bottom, and anyone able to dive to the bottom of the ocean could get into it, even though the Tartar waters run right by the entrance.

"You mean Tartrar?" specified Davkaleon.

"It is in your Daeya where it is called Tartrar. In the Adoleseet depository, it is called Tartar."

"Right, right, go on." Davkaleon did not argue, especially since in the jeweler Piromis' manuscripts Tartrar was also called the Tartar. Similar names for the same place.

"The first cave is not always linked to mages," Chapius said.

"Yeah, I know. All the sportsmen swim into it. In any case, all the students of Master Gandall do this," agreed Davkaleon.

"The rest of the caves are more difficult. Only those who are somehow connected with magic can get into them. The easiest way to get to the hidden caves is to come to the second cave. For this, it is not necessary to undergo the initiation ceremony. I'm not sure, but it doesn't seem even necessary to have a magician-mentor. In my opinion, the potion is quite sufficient."

"You don't need even the potion. I think that I occurred in that cave when I was trying to get the jeweler Piromis' note. My brothers were with me. They never drank the potion of mages," answered Davkaleon.

"So, I understood everything correctly," Chapius rejoiced. "I found the following description of the Chamber of Neophytes in the depository of Adolees."

1. Visible Cave:

The entrance is open to all who dare.

2. Secret caves:

a) The entrance is open to neophytes before their initiation.

b) The entrance is open to neophytes after their initiation.

"Let's find the Chamber of Neophytes; we'll see what's there, and then we'll try to find the Chamber of Mages, it definitely should be there," Chapius said.

Although it did not follow from Chapius' description that the Chamber of Mages was located in the Cliff Rock, finding the Chamber of Neophytes was also an interesting task.

"Tartar flows at the entrance to the visible cave. Moreover, the word 'flows' is not a very good term, because Tartar rushes like mad. Are you sure you can handle it?" Davkaleon asked.

Chapius proudly straightened his shoulders and put his leg forward. "Of course, I do! Have you forgotten that you are talking to a fire-breathing Dragon?!" He wore a proud, fierce expression.

"But still, stay close to me. It would be a shame if Tartar transforms you into a cutlet," said Davkaleon, who loved Chapius.

When they reached the rock, they both jumped down. Descending into the cave, they found a disguised entrance to the secret room, just as Davkaleon did when searching for Piromis' note. There was a DRAGON sign on one of the walls. His last time here, Davkaleon had pulled out an envelope with a note from the jeweler. "As far as I understand, this is a room in the cave, into which the entrance is open to the students of the Mages before their initiation. You and I did not go through initiation. How do we get to the next chamber?"

They walked around the room carefully examining everything around. They found no markings except the DRAGON sign.

"Let me go and look," Chapius suggested, touching the sign. He looked in and even whispered something, but it did not help.

"Maybe you should introduce yourself?" proposed Davkaleon and, looking inside, announced: "I Dav..." He didn't finish. Chapius pulled his hand, and Davkaleon remembered that in the temple in the rock, where his acquaintance with the Mages began, he called himself Alfreydon.

"I'm Alfreydon," he announced.

Nothing had changed in the room.

"ChapiusCloyAlfreyDon," pronounced Chapius.

The secret safe from which Davkaleon once got the jeweler's note grew in size. Davkaleon and Chapius found themselves inside it. There were no doors or windows. There were no signs either.

"No matter how many times I faced the creations of the mages, they all wanted a taste of blood," Davkaleon said. He smiled grimly and pricked his finger with a dagger.

Blood drops fell on the floor, but the entrance-exit did not appear.

"Probably it was not sufficient," Davkaleon said and pricked himself again.

Nothing changed in the room.

"Now you try," Davkaleon offered to Chapius.

It didn't help either.

"Let's do it at the same time."

Alas!

"Blood doesn't help," Chapius sighed after a few minutes. "Let's think about what to do."

"A pair of chairs would be nice for pondering," Davkaleon remarked.

"You'll do without chairs," somebody's voice sounded. "What did you come for?"

"We missed you," Davkaleon said.

"What, are you, nuts?" Chapius slapped his forehead, then turned and said, "Dear Lord, will you let us enter the Chamber of Neophytes?"

"And what the hell you forgot there?" asked the voice he'd called *Dear Lord*.

"We want to get acquainted," Chapius continued.

"Oh, you want to get acquainted?" the voice asked with obvious sarcasm. "And where are your rings of Neophytes?"

"Rings of Neophytes?" asked Chapius.

"We left them at home," Davkaleon said.

"So, you're also scatterbrains." The voice laughed. "And what level of neophytes, would you wish to make happy with your presence?"

"The highest, of course," Davkaleon said.

"What are you talking about? Oh, what joy! Well, you

are always welcome! Enter the keys, just don't make a mistake, otherwise you will pop out," the voice warned.

Something resembling a table appeared in front of Davkaleon and Chapius. It depicted a series of numbers from 1 to 9 and then from 9 to 1. There were two rectangles under the numbers. A button with the digit "1" was located under each figure.

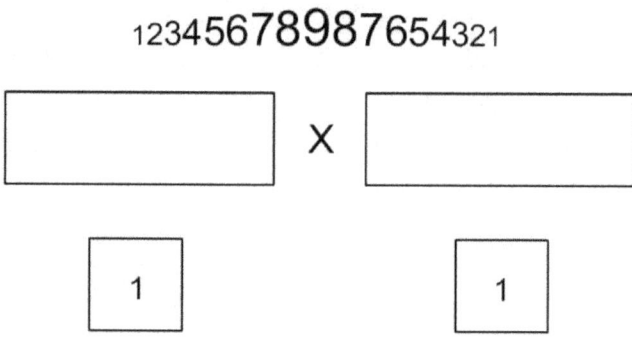

"You said you wanted to get to the highest level of neophytes. For neophytes, the highest level is seventh. We should enter the number seven," suggested Chapius.

"That won't work. Only *ones* are acceptable here."

Davkaleon tried to press the button with figure one. The number "1" appeared in the top rectangle. Davkaleon pressed again. A second "1" appeared in the same rectangle.

"What should we do? Let me press four times, and then you press three. In total there will be seven," suggested Davkaleon.

"What kind of jerks want to find their way to neophytes?" the voice commented, clearly unimpressed.

"Maybe each of us should enter 3 and a half to get a

total of 7?" Chapius launched the idea.

"3 and a half will not work. How do you enter "half"? There are only ones here," objected Davkaleon.

"Blockheads! So, what did you decide? What codes will you enter? It doesn't really matter, of course. You're about to pop out into the Tartar..."

"Wait please," said Davkaleon. "We will guess right now."

"You have 10 seconds," the voice replied.

"Listen, there are two of us. Each of us must press the button seven times!" Davkaleon suggested.

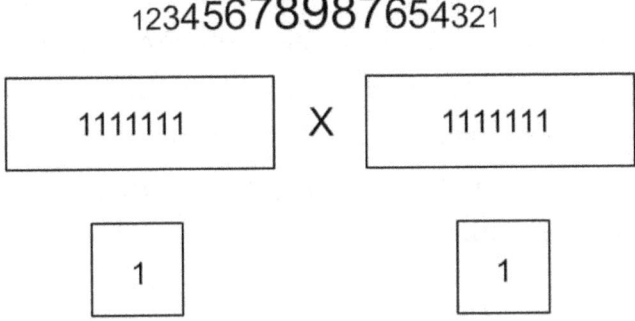

"Are you sure?" Chapius asked doubtfully. "Look, there's another unknown X between the rectangles. Do you know what it is equal to?"

"Press the button; the time is expiring!" Davkaleon insisted, beginning to worry.

After seven *ones* appeared in each of the rectangles, the voice went silent for a few seconds. Then they heard the question: "Is that all? Have you finished?"

The question made Davkaleon prick up ears. He felt that they were expected to act further, but he was not sure which actions they had to do.

Chapius did not hesitate. "Of course!" he declared.

They spun in place for a long time, but finally, they ended up where they were promised—in the Tartar. Davkaleon believed that he had learned to cope well with Tartar, Now, he learned that this was far from the case. They were twisted and flung like feathers. The current carried them at a breakneck speed.

At first, Davkaleon grabbed Chapius by the hand and held him. But this risked being simultaneously pulled into some kind of funnel or slammed against stones. Suddenly, Davkaleon felt that something or someone was pulling him up. It took him a long time to climb. He was gasping for breath when a blue strip of sky appeared high in the distance. They surfaced in the middle of the ocean. Huge waves were raging all around. Neither the shores nor the Cliff Rock could be seen. Looking at Chapius, Davkaleon realized who was pulling him up. Chapius had not only grown gills for himself but also pumped himself with air. Now, he was slowly swaying on the waves. Chapius, it seems, even liked it; in any case, a blissful smile shone on his face.

"You look like a balloon," Davkaleon said.

Chapius replied, "We should get to Neophytes' cave again. This is such a *great* workout. In Adolees, they charge crazy money for such things. True, they give me a discount, but even at a lower price, it's a lot. And here you are thrown into Tartar for free! If I speak about it in Adolees, no one will believe me."

"Into the cave? Do you want to go back to the cave?

Right now?"

Davkaleon's head kept... fizzing. He expected that Chapius would not be in the best shape, but Chapius continued to express his enjoyment. "This is so brilliant! I managed to grow gills in time and figured out how to escape from Tartar! This is the way the participants of the Grand Prize are trained in Adolees. The dream of any Adoleeseet is to become a participant in this game. During the game, participants can find themselves in the ocean, and on fire, and even in the crater of an active volcano. Their life depends on the speed with which they turn into someone who can survive there."

"Chapius, did it ever occur to you that, unlike you, I can't grow gills for myself?"

"Exactly! You cannot! I didn't think about that. I will need to search in our Adolees' depository for how to grow artificial gills." Chapius continued to muse about what needed to be done to help Davkaleon go on an excursion to the erupting volcano and soak up a lava bath.

"Chapius, a lava bath sounds tempting, but it will wait. In the meantime, I'd prefer you to soar since you can grow wings at will and look in which direction we should swim to the shore."

"Oh, Davkaleon, I tell you such cool things, and you're so boring. Isn't any of this interesting to you?" Chapius frowned but rose into the air. "We're going to swim this way," he said after a few minutes.

Chapter 4. Rings of Neophytes

Davkaleon would have preferred to rest before returning to the cave of Neophytes. Who knew where they'd end up next time? Davkaleon had no doubt that without the rings of Neophytes, they wouldn't be allowed anywhere. But he did not want to admit it, so they ended up in the cave again.

Before going to the secret room, they decided to try to crack the puzzle first.

"I don't understand what the unknown X between the rectangles should be equal to. Could it be equal to anything? Chapius asked.

Davkaleon was puzzled by Chapius' question.

"Unknown X? Where did you find it?"

"I mean the big X that was between the rectangles," Chapius replied, surprised that Davkaleon did not notice the big X sign.

"Chapius, maybe this is not an unknown X at all but the sign for multiplication."

"The sign for multiplication? In your Daeya, does the X stands for multiplication?" asked Chapius. He slapped himself. "Exactly! When we learned to count in the first grade, we also used *X*. It was later, when we started to learn how to compile scripts, that we began to denote multiplication in these scripts with an asterisk," Chapius recalled.

"Scripts? Are you taught to write scripts? Like the mages?" Davkaleon remembered talking about scripts with the mages' students in the temple in the rock.

"No, no, what are you saying? I have a lot to learn before I can write a mages' script. I can only compile very simple codes," replied Chapius.

"But you can learn it, and you don't have to be a Mage to do that?" asked Davkaleon.

"Of course!" Chapius answered with conviction.

"If that X stood for multiplication, then let's multiply and see what we'll get. Each of us pressed '1' seven times.

$$\underbrace{1111111}_{7} \times \underbrace{1111111}_{7} = 1234567654321$$

"Look at what I came up with!" exclaimed Davkaleon in a minute. "Let's check what would happen if each of us pressed "1" nine times.

$$\underbrace{111111111}_{9} \times \underbrace{111111111}_{9} = 12345678987654321$$

"That is the same 12345678987654321 as on the wall! It's so simple! This is what we were asked! And we, like the last dummies, couldn't guess it! Off to the secret room!"

A few minutes later, the following table appeared in front of them:

$1 \times 1 = \mathbf{1}$

$\underbrace{11}_{2} \times \underbrace{11}_{2} = 1\mathbf{2}1$

$\underbrace{111}_{3} \times \underbrace{111}_{3} = 12\mathbf{3}21$

$\underbrace{1111}_{4} \times \underbrace{1111}_{4} = 123\mathbf{4}321$

$\underbrace{11111}_{5} \times \underbrace{11111}_{5} = 1234\mathbf{5}4321$

$\underbrace{111111}_{6} \times \underbrace{111111}_{6} = 12345\mathbf{6}54321$

$\underbrace{1111111}_{7} \times \underbrace{1111111}_{7} = 123456\mathbf{7}654321$

$\underbrace{11111111}_{8} \times \underbrace{11111111}_{8} = 1234567\mathbf{8}7654321$

$\underbrace{111111111}_{9} \times \underbrace{111111111}_{9} = 12345678\mathbf{9}87654321$

"You know, I'm surprised they didn't kill us in the cave instead of throwing us into the Tartrar. It's so simple," Davkaleon lamented. "Look, the largest digit in the number, the one in the middle, indicates how many 'ones' should be in each rectangle."

"Any puzzle seems simple when you solve it," Chapius

consoled his friend.

*****

Adamant and Ecktoral played their fantastic chess.

Davkaleon and Chapius appeared on the screen in front of them in the familiar Chamber of Neophytes.

"Look, your protégés have already showed up. It wasn't even a week after they finished with multiplication. Before you know it, they will cope with fractions. Do you still intend to drag them to Twierks?" Adamant chuckled.

"Don't be sarcastic. They will learn." Ecktoral smiled. "And much more quickly than you think!"

*****

"You're back again? Didn't you forget the Neophytes' rings?" said the voice.

"We were in such a hurry that we did not go home to get the rings. However, this time we do not want to try to get to neophytes of the highest level. The initial level will be fine for us," Davkaleon said.

"What?! You didn't go home for the rings? You have no idea what the ring of Neophyte is! And how could HE HIMSELF take you as disciples?"

Scenes of Davkaleon and Chapius being swept by the Tartrar into the ocean popped before their eyes in the air. They overheard their own conversation when Chapius raved about the workout he had received.

"Well, well, you do have some positive attributes. I think I understood why HE took you as disciples, but your knowledge isn't a penny-worth, so you must learn and

31

learn."

"Dear Lord, don't throw us out. Will you be so generous ..." Chapius started but did not finish.

"I *won't*," snapped the voice. "If you came here counting on my generosity, then you had better disappear from here and never come back."

"I rely on my knowledge," Chapius answered quickly.

"Knowledge? Was it thanks to your knowledge that you could not do a simple multiplication?" the invisible lord burst out laughing.

"We guessed, though not the first time," Davkaleon interjected. "We just didn't notice that there was a multiplication sign."

"Well, I see, you are a fan of arguing. Please note that today's attempt is your *last* one. If you don't answer, you won't come in here again."

"And if we do answer, we'll get the rings of Neophytes?" Davkaleon asked.

"First answer and we'll see."

"Right, right," Davkaleon didn't argue this time.

"Let's see how you are doing with this little puzzle."

A table desk appeared in front of Davkaleon and Chapius. Something like a papyrus and a pencil lay on it.

"Listen to the task," said the voice.

16 soldiers are required along the walls of the square bastion.

The captain placed the soldiers so that there were 5 of them on each side.

Then the colonel came and ordered the soldiers to be placed so that there were 6 of them on each side.

After the colonel, the general came and placed the soldiers, 7 people on each side.

Show me how the captain, colonel and general have placed the soldiers.

"I know I know!" Davkaleon yelled happily, unable to contain his excitement.

Similar tasks were often put in his military school. This was a simple one. At school, they asked much more difficult ones.

"Well, if you know, then answer," ordered the invisible interlocutor.

Davkaleon was never a good artist, but he painted the answers just fine.

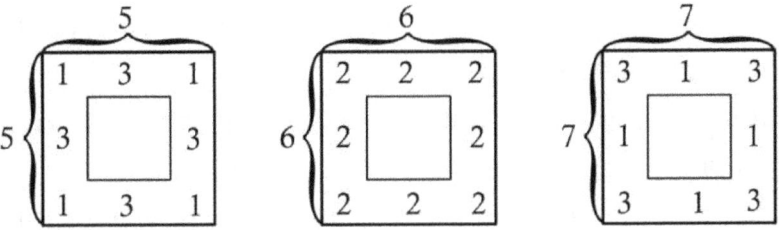

"All right, get your rings," said the Lord of the Chamber of Neophytes. Simple black hoops appeared on the table desk.

"May these curiosities somehow be connected with magic?" Davkaleon was surprised but said nothing.

Davkaleon glanced at Chapius, who looked somewhat confused as well.

"What are you waiting for? Put on them!" The voice ordered.

They wondered how to put the hoops on. They were too big to be rings and too small to be bracelets.

"How long should I wait on you two?" the voice asked impatiently.

Davkaleon and Chapius together put the hoops on their fingers, aware that the hoops would inevitably fly off. But the hoops didn't fly off. Instead, they started to shrink right before their eyes. A few moments later, the ring of Neophyts tightly wrapped Davkaleon's finger. The second ring did the same with Chapius' finger. But that was only the beginning. The rings began to fade—thinning before their eyes.

"What happened to the rings?" Davkaleon asked.

"What??? You don't know that either? Have a nice trip!" The voice said, and the invisible Lord threw them out.

This time they flew a fair distance before falling into the fire raging underneath.

"Dammit," Davkaleon cursed, knowing that he would likely burn.

Once again, he was saved by Chapius. Grabbing Davkaleon, Chapius flew away.

"What a heavy guy you are," Chapius complained when they landed in some unknown place.

Davkaleon had bitter thoughts. "So, it turns out that without Chapius, I can't get to any magical places." He felt ill at ease. Adventure and danger were his element. Saving others really fascinated him. And today? Both times *he was saved by Chapius!* He might have gotten out of Tartar on his own, even though the air supply was tight, but in the flame, he would have been dead meat.

Chapius must have been thinking the same. "I will look in the Adolees Knowledge depository for instructions on how to travel for those who cannot mutate. There are many of these in Adolees. Why should they be forced to stay in one place?"

"Do you think it's possible?" Davkaleon asked hopefully.

"This is probably what is called *magic* in Daeya, and *science* in Adolees," Chapius replied.

"Don't you in Adolees believe in magic at all?" Davkaleon was surprised.

"There is not even such a word in the Adolees' language. I first heard it from you in Daeya," replied Chapius.

"Let's speak not of magic, but of witchcraft or enchantment."

"No," Chapius shook his head.

"How then do you explain everything supernatural?"

"What is this 'supernatural'?" asked Chapius.

"The things and events which you cannot explain or do not understand how that can be. For example, a mysterious voice in the cave. There was nobody there except us, but someone was talking to us. If this is magic, then everything is clear. Magic can do anything. If, as you say, there is no magic, then who was he?"

"It's simple," replied Chapius. "They hid tiny video cameras somewhere in the room and saw us perfectly."

"What's a video camera?" Davkaleon asked.

"My sisters have a video camera at home. You should see them twirl around in front of it, showing off to each other. You would immediately understand everything. Next time, I will steal this thing from them for a few hours and bring it to you to show what it is. But I must steal the camera surreptitiously, or they'll make a fuss. Believe me, a meeting with the Great DRAGON of Adolees will seem a trifle compared to my angry sisters."

"Wouldn't it be better to ask them? As you'll return this camera back to them."

"To ask? What are you saying? They won't give it up. They cannot live a day without their camera."

"Well, let's say these video cameras are installed in the cave, and someone is sitting somewhere and waiting until it pops into our head to attend the cave..."

"Come on, Davkaleon, no one is waiting for us anywhere purposefully. There are sensors in the cave that respond, for example, to movement."

"Sensors?" asked Davkaleon not knowing what Chapius is talking about.

"These are devices that respond to motion or sound. An artificial robot or artificial intellect. If you want, I'll bring you a book about robots next time."

"How am I going to read it?" Davkaleon asked. "It's in the Adolees' language."

"With the help of the Neophytes' ring. It'll translate everything for you," replied Chapius. "But don't ask me how. I do not know yet."

"Look in your depository for information on how to get artificial gills, and also how to protect yourself from fire. As for me, I'll visit Elfid. My brother, for certain will find in his manuscripts something about the rings of Neophytes and tell us where they went."

Chapter 5. Conversation with Elfid

"The Chamber of Neophytes? Have you and Chapius visited it?" Elfid was impressed.

Davkaleon's brother even jumped up from his chair and walked around the room in excitement.

"You see, I've been trying to figure out how to get into this Chamber for a long time," Elfid explained. "It's the only possible way to pass the mages' exam for those who did not attend magic school. In none of the manuscripts I have found a description of how to get into this Chamber, but now it is clear that it is in the Cliff Rock. Anyone who can dive to the bottom can swim into the cave at the foot of the cliff. Unfortunately, this method will not work for me," Elfid sighed. "I'm not able to live without air for that long."

"You will be! I'll have you there in no time," Davkaleon said. "I will jump into the Tartar Falls. We'll be in a cave within minutes."

"And how will you get back? The waterfall of Tartrar will not help us to climb," Elfid smiled sadly and added, "But this is not the only point. Remember, when you first brought Chapius to me, we had a conversation about initiation. I confessed to you then that I had failed my initiation."

"Elfid, how could this happen? I have never met a person in my life who would know more than you!"

"I didn't fail initiation because I didn't know something. I knew everything that was required and even more. The fact is that I was *scared* doomed me. This is unacceptable for a future mage. They do not admit to initiation for the second time."

"So why do you refuse help?" Davkaleon was surprised. "The waterfall will instantly bring you down. Don't worry, I'll be holding you. As for the ascent to the top? For that, we need Chapius. He will instantly turn into some kind of fish and jump out. I assure you, he will be completely delighted and tell you that in Adolees, you'd have to pay crazy money for such training. In Daeya, you can get such a benefit for free. He has already shared this with me. Again and again."

"The Chamber of Neophytes will not let in it the one who used someone's help to get in it. I need to figure out how to get there myself," explained Elfid.

"What do you know about the Rings of Neophytes?" asked Davkaleon

"The Ring of Neophytes is a kind of a key. If you have it, then in places where neophytes are allowed to attend, you should not give your name. The teacher's name is also not required. In your case, you possibly do not need to drink the mages' potion," explained Elfid.

The conversation was interrupted by a knock on the door. A messenger handed Elfid an envelope. The envelope contained a document authorizing a visit to the secret section of the library. Elfid smiled broadly.

"What is that department?" Davkaleon asked.

"This is a department in which manuscripts that cover forbidden things are collected."

"Do you mean …?"

Davkaleon almost uttered the word "Twierks." He resisted. In Daeya, it was forbidden to talk about Twierks.

"Including this," smiled Elfid.

"How did you manage to get such permission?" Davkaleon asked.

"I wrote a rationale in which I argued that all permitted sources somehow related to discrepancies with divine predictions have long been studied by the priests. Prohibited manuscripts can provide a hint."

"And the priests agreed?"

"Not right away. The Council of Priests considered my application *nine times*. Each time, the priests demanded further evidence that the forbidden manuscripts could help to find out something new. The last time, I was asked to indicate a manuscript as an example. When I asked them how I could specify the manuscript if I had not read it, they replied that I was summoned to the council. Not to ask questions, but to answer them. During the first vote, the number of priests was even. Half for, half against.

Then someone else was invited. This someone abstained and was replaced, but that did not help. The newly arrived priest also abstained!"

"This sounds very political," Davkaleon said.

Elfid took a deep breath before continuing. "It was agreed before the last vote that there should be no abstentions, and each member of the Council should throw a black or white ball. In the end, it turned out that five balls were white, five were black, and one was green. Where the green ball came from and what it meant remains a mystery. The Council retired for a short three-month meeting, but finally decided to grant my request."

"Wow! Now you can figure out how to get there; you yourself know where," Davkaleon said with admiration.

Elfid put the envelope on the table, and a card fell out of it. The word "Invitation," written in red ink, immediately caught the eye.

"Where are you invited to?" Davkaleon asked.

"To Llill on the Day of Ivana-Kupala," answered Elfid.

"What kind of holiday is this?" Davkaleon, who had never heard of such an event, was surprised.

"It's Summer Sun Celebration," Elfid said without further details.

"Wait, wait," Davkaleon insisted, "the holiday of the shortest night was a few days ago."

"Yes, it was," agreed Elfid, "but in Llill, several holidays are celebrated, one after the other. They begin with the holiday of the shortest night of Lit, smoothly move on to celebrate the longest day or the day of Svarog and end with Kupala."

40

"Everyone in Daeya knows about the holidays of Lit and Svarog, but I have never heard of Kupala," Davkaleon disagreed and turned over the invitation card. On the reverse side, there was a description of the Kupala feast.

"What? Witchcraft? Night festivities? A Magic Fern blossom? A play at the Llill's temple? And you didn't tell me about that?" Davkaleon was indignant.

Elfid tried to take the ticket, but Davkaleon at that time read: "Elfid is invited with a guest."

"Who do you want to invite?" Davkaleon asked.

"Well, there you are. I assume you'd like to go," Elfid sighed.

"Of course, I would! Why not? Have you invited someone?"

"I haven't invited anyone yet, and I'll hardly invite anyone, but the fact is that you should not be at this holiday."

"Why?" Davkaleon was taken aback.

Elfid took a manuscript describing the Kupala feast from the table and showed Davkaleon a place that said that during this holiday one can get to Twierks.

"And you didn't want to tell me about it?" Davkaleon demanded.

"You yourself told me that during Walpurgis Night, the temple in the rock threw you out to the ruins of the Black Castle and forbade you to appear for a year. If you break the prohibition, the entrance will be closed to you forever," explained Elfid.

"But I will be your guest, and you are invited! It does not say that the guest is not allowed to enter! On the contrary, it says that the guest is invited."

"Do you understand that you risks here?" asked Elfid.

"Even if they catch me, we will bluff it out!" Davkaleon boasted. "You don't have to know that the temple forbade me to appear during a year. And I have no idea about Kupala and about places where one can get during this holiday."

"All right." Elfid waved his hand. "That's up to you."

"What is this magic fern flower?" Davkaleon asked. "I've never heard of that."

"Let's use my permission to visit the secret section of the library and talk there," Elfid suggested.

"Can I go in there, too?"

"You cannot enter the department itself, but there is a guest room. I can invite you there."

Having strayed along the corridors-passages of the school of Sciences, they found themselves in a small granite room. Davkaleon recalled the story of his Adoleeseet friend Chapius that granite is the most reliable material that protects thoughts from scanning.

"Are you interested in the fern flower? There are many disputes about it. No one in Daeya knows what is true. The fact is that the fern in Daeya grows but never blooms. Some sources claim that in the old days the fern bloomed, and then for some reason it gave over. The manuscripts of the Llill's sorcerers say that the fern blooms in Twierks. On the night of Kupala, the flower is shown in Daeya for a moment. This happens exactly at midnight. If you have time to pick a flower, then further you have a chance to get your hands on the magic itself. True, no manuscript or handwriting really explains what exactly this magic is. But they all agree that the chance to benefit from this magic is close to zero, and the probability that you will lose your head is almost one hundred percent."

"If it were that gloomy, there would hardly be anyone wishing to possess the flower," Davkaleon grinned.

"You be the judge," smiled Elfid. "Some myths claim that magic can endow you with unprecedented abilities. However, they do not say which ones. Others promise that whatever you desire will be granted. The most generous prophesy the fulfillment of three wishes. The legends of the Llill's sorcerers say that picking a flower will bring you to Twierks. Local inhabitants consider the flower as their property, which the impudent newcomer stole from them. The inhabitants of Twierks do not differ in meekness, so deadly dances, fiery swords, and meetings with evil spirits happen at the end of the feast. There are many legends, and they are all different, but you get the idea."

"Can we talk here about the place where the flower grows without fear of arrest?" asked Davkaleon.

"Yes, no one will hear you here," nodded Elfid.

"If I find myself in Twierks, how will I find Twerks' Llill?" Davkaleon asked.

"I don't know that," Elfid threw up his hands, "but if you are interested in Twierks' Llill because of your desire to find Heather who you like, then on the night of Kupala, she will most likely be in the Magical Forest. You'll get in it anyway...if only Twierks lets you.

*****

Davkaleon entered his room. There was a scroll on the table. Expanding it, Davkaleon saw a long list of tasks.

"What? Who has nothing better to do than leave their tasks on my desk?" Davkaleon quickly rolled up the scroll.

"You can roll me up as much as you want, but until you solve all the tasks, the second portion of them will not appear," Davkaleon heard someone's voice.

"Who are you?" he was taken aback.

"Not who, but what. I am your assignment. The first one. There will be many of us. Until you solve all, you will *not* be able to use the Neophyte ring."

Chapter 6. Fern Flower

"You will have fun, and I, in your opinion, should be bored? No, we are flying together," said Davkaleon's dragon Aleurh when Davkaleon told him about the Kupala night.

"Don't be offended," Davkaleon said, feeling a little guilty. "Elfid may invite only one guest to the Magical Forest."

"I don't care about a forest with flowers," Aleurh shrugged his shoulders, "You think I can't find a dragoness in Llill?"

"I'm sure you can. It seems that all Llill has gathered here," Davkaleon remarked, looking at the huge crowd in front of the temple.

The residents of Llill liked to celebrate. Holidays almost never stopped. When did locals have time to work? A melodic voice sounded nearby:

Pay, handsome boy, for fortune telling.
Give me a gold dreamboat boy.
Present your palm, I'll tell the fortune.
About your desired girl.

Davkaleon turned around. A young black-eyed girl beckoned him with her finger. "Cutie," she said, "I know everything about you. Give me a gold coin, and I'll tell you who your heart yearns for, I'll tell you when you meet her, and I'll portend what awaits you ahead."

Davkaleon put on a smile. Although he had a high opinion of himself, no one had yet called him "Cutie." He liked it. The black-eyed girl came closer and showed four cards. Queens of spades, clubs, diamonds, and hearts smiled at Davkaleon.

"Do you see her?" asked the black-eyed fortune teller, flapping cards in front of Davkaleon's eyes.

Three cards suddenly disappeared, and Heather was looking at him from the fourth one. She was wearing a mask and was saying something to him. "Do you want to hear what your honey-flower says to you? Give me a gold coin, and you'll hear."

Without hesitation, Davkaleon pulled out a gold coin and handed it to the fortune-teller, and the card began to speak. "Alfreydon, where are you?" She knew him as Alfreydon, not Davkaleon. "You are so brave and strong. You saved me from the terrible monsters! Will you be in the Magic Forest today?"

"Of course, I will! I came on purpose!"

"She doesn't hear you," said the fortune-teller. "Give me one more gold coin, and your girl will hear you."

Davkaleon handed the required coin to the fortune-teller. "I'll be near the nearest fern," she said, "but don't linger, otherwise I'll be scared.'

"Give me ten coins, and you can talk to her without hindrance," suggested the fortune-teller.

"You've got your coins already," Elfid said indignantly.

"No, no, Elfid, I will pay!" Davkaleon pulled out a handful of coins. The last thing he wanted was to give up talking with Heather because of some lousy gold!

"You are such a great warrior! I've never met a man like you," Heather's voice chirped. "You are the best of the best!"

Davkaleon could listen to such a speech for hours—especially from Heather. The fortune-teller, meanwhile, again asked for gold.

"Do you know how hard it is to keep a conversation between you? I'll have to rest for three days after this!" she complained.

Elfid interrupted. "Say no more!! Find someone else!"

"Why are you so greedy?" the fortune-teller shouted to Elfid. "You men! You gather together, hunt, get a free lunch. What should I do? What sort of hunter could I be? I must pay for everything! For food, for firewood, for fire. I am a lonely girl. There is no one to intercede for me. A cold bed awaits me at home. I am starving and homeless in the middle of a snowstorm."

"What a snowstorm?! Where did you find the blizzard in the middle of summer?" Elfid was indignant.

"And in winter?" the fortune-teller said, nearly in tears.

Davkaleon felt such sympathy for the girl that, despite the warmth, he felt snowflakes on his face.

Elfid said something about the summer heat. What heat? Davkaleon felt wet snow and chilly cold.

"Ten coins are nothing," he said and pulled a handful of coins from his pocket. "I won this much at cards yesterday."

"You didn't win yesterday, you lost!" Aleurh the dragon said. "And this morning you were rushing from one creditor to another."

Something glimmered in Davkaleon's mind. Aleurh was right. He did meet with creditors today. He wanted to know what for. Probably, in order to repay a debt!

"Leave here!" said Aleurh to the fortune-teller.

"I can leave," the girl grinned and showed the card. Davkaleon saw Heather holding a small white kitten in her arms. Next to her stood a brute guy with a huge black cat. Davkaleon rushed forward.

"*Auferte*," said Elfid.

"You're heartless! Will you deprive a poor girl of her earnings ?!" the fortune-teller squealed. With a wave of her hand, she threw a handful of flickering small stones. Whirling stones drifted down, but before they reached the ground, they dissolved into the air. Davkaleon and Aleurh looked in amazement at the disappearing reflections.

"*Auferte quod discuteret.*" Elfid shouted.

"You're soulless! You won't see the Magic Forest today! You won't rip off the magic flower today!" said the fortune-teller walking away. The snow, cold, and shimmering stones disappeared along with her.

"These vanished stones are similar to the one you won about a month ago," Aleurh said. "You still have it?"

Digging in his pockets, Davkaleon pulled out a beautiful iridescent stone.

"Opal, the stone of deceptive hopes," said Elfid examining the stone.

"So that's why your luck has turned away from you," said Aleurh. "Throw it out immediately!"

"Is it really a stone of deceptive hopes?" Davkaleon asked.

"That's what they call it," said Elfid.

"Does that mean we won't get into the Magic Forest?"

Davkaleon was upset.

"The fortune-teller threw imaginative opals, so if you believe in her threats, then I won't get into the Magic Forest," Elfid chuckled. "As for you, we spoke already that on this Kupala night. You won't be able to get there."

"The fortune teller threw these opals at you, but they touched me too," Davkaleon sighed.

"You're very gullible," his brother replied. "Fortune-tellers sense clients like that from a distance. If I hadn't stopped her, you would have given her everything."

"But she showed me Heather," Davkaleon said.

"No, she showed you four cards. Everything else you imagined yourself," said Elfid.

"There's no way that I imagined that! I heard what Heather was saying. She said all the right things!"

"What about yesterday's game?" Aleurh asked.

Davkaleon sighed. He'd already remembered that part. He'd nearly lost his shirt!

"You have to learn to resist compulsion," said Elfid. "You see what the fortune-teller did to you? If this becomes known, you will have to put an end to your dreams of becoming Commander-In-Chief."

Someone was hanging around Davkaleon's leg. Looking down, Davkaleon saw a small striped animal, resembling Heather's kitten, but bigger. Reddish-black stripes glittered beautifully in the bright light of three moons. The little animal jumped on one of the trees growing nearby and instantly climbed up.

"Where did the trees come from?" Davkaleon was surprised. "We were in the square in front of the temple."

Davkaleon looked around. The temple disappeared. The square in front of it vanished, too. There were trees and glades everywhere. The river was visible not far away. Wreaths were floating along it. Bonfires blazed on the shore.

A voice came out of nowhere. "If you want, you can take a walk in the Magic Forest. If you are lucky enough to see a fern flower, do not forget to make a wish before picking the flower. And keep in mind, you can pick a flower exactly at midnight, and, moreover, only one! You'll have only one minute at your disposal. Then move away from the fern quickly, or the Magic Forest won't let you go. And even if you manage to come back, your soul will remain there. However, this does not apply to those who received an invitation on Kupala holiday, as well as their guests. These lucky ones are safe in the Magic Forest on Kupala Night. But they must also leave the Forest before the first light of day."

Pleasant music began to sound, and laughing girls in wreaths appeared in the forest meadow.

"Let's do guesswork?" suggested one of them and threw a wreath into the river.

"If you want to guess, then first you have to jump over the fire," answered another.

"I don't really like fortune-telling with bonfires. Where could one find good dragon ale here? And where have all the dragonesses gone?" grumbled Aleurh.

It did not take long to see young dragonesses. Dragon drinks appeared under thick foliage. Rapturous Aleurh immediately went to them.

"Are you going to dragonesses or for drinks?" Davkaleon asked.

"Both" Aleurh waved his paw goodbye.

"You shouldn't try to pick the flower," Elfid reminded.

"But everyone can get there for one minute," objected Davkaleon.

Davkaleon hasn't yet seen the fern bloom, but he wished to pick the flower. Then his wish will come true. Which one? He wanted to get into Twierks, but not for one minute or even ten. It's more accurate to say that he wanted to find a way to Twierks which he could use at any time. In Twierks, of course, he would find Heather, but after that, he would go to the mages' depository. In addition, he wanted to find the missing jeweler's manuscripts, and then the magic jewelry itself. However, that's not all. There is also a lost path to the city of the gods, and Davkaleon wouldn't mind finding it. And he also had to visit the "*Tender Monster*" and find out what the aira is. It seems he wanted a large number of things. How to express all this in a single wish?

While Davkaleon was thinking how to cram a few different desires into one, the reddish-black animal jumped from a tree and ran in the direction of the white fluffy clump. The clump straightened and arched its back. Davkaleon rushed after it. The kitten passed one fern bush, ran past another, and disappeared behind a blazing fire. Davkaleon went around the fire, but the kitten was gone. Instead, he saw a bright growing ruby-colored bud that looked alive. The bud grew in size before his eyes. Probably, it was midnight because the flower was blooming. The flower burned like a hot coal, illuminating everything around with its flame. A strong heat came from the plant.

"How to rip it off? It'll burn everything if you touch it," Davkaleon's thought. He took a dragon-skin glove from his pocket.

"A wish! A wish must be conceived!" a thought went through his head.

But he didn't have time to conceive a wish. He heard the name *Alfreydon* sounded near him. It could only have been Heather. Davkaleon lunged forward, but Heather was not there. She was not behind him either.

"What's the matter with me?! Girls should be given flowers!" Davkaleon slapped himself on the forehead and touched the scarlet flower.

An unknown force jerked him up, twisted, whirled, and flung him away.

"How dare you enter Twierks?! Have you forgotten that you're not allowed to get here for a year!?! For that ..."

"No, no, no!" Davkaleon squirmed. "I didn't want to enter Twierks, I just wanted to pick a flower!"

"And where is the flower, in your opinion? Not in Twierks?" the voice was malicious.

"But I didn't know," Davkaleon tried to get out of it.

"Oh, you didn't know?" sarcasm was clearly heard in the voice.

The ghostly figures of Elfid and Davkaleon appeared in the air.

"You yourself told me that during Walpurgis Night, the temple in the rock threw you out to the ruins of the Black

Castle and forbade you to appear for a year. If you break the ban, the entrance will be closed to you forever," the voice of imaginary Elfid sounded.

"Even if they catch me, we will get out!" The impudent voice of imaginary Davkaleon answered with conviction. *"You don't have to know that the temple forbade me to appear during the year. And I have no idea about Kupala and places you can get during this holiday."*

"Wait, do not block his entrance forever," said the very real Elfid. "I had to explain him things better."

"You did," came the displeased voice.

"But that was the first time he heard about the Magic Forest and about the fern flower."

"The last time he grabbed a weapon in the temple. This time, he heard about the Twierks' flower. Does one have to explain it to him ten times?"

"But he doesn't live in Twierks permanently. His teacher doesn't even let him go there. It's hard to get used to Twierks."

"Okay," the voice said. "Keep in mind that you are using my leniency for the last time. If you dare to return to Twierks in the next three years, I will kick you out forever!"

"Three years? As many as three?!" Davkaleon was indignant, but Elfid grabbed his hand and squeezed his mouth.

Aleurh was outraged. "And what am I to be punished for? I wouldn't get into that Twierks of yours even for free! I am good in Daeya!"

"Yes? You wouldn't get there? Who picked two flowers?!!

You've all been warned that you can pick one flower only!"

"And if there were two dragonesses with me?!" Aleurh argued. "I am a polite dragon! One flower for one dragoness, the other for another!"

Instead of answering, the whirlwind hurled them all towards the caves of Llill.

*****

In a room with no doors or windows...

"As I understand it, Twierks threw him out for three years so he wouldn't meet Heather ahead of time," Adamant remarked.

"Naturally," Ecktoral nodded. "They are still too young to date. Davkaleon for the present is a boy, not ready for the tournament."

"I got the idea," Adamant chuckled. "You're going to show him Heather from time to time and arrange a brief meeting in the finest canons of romantic drama. For three years, Davkaleon will fight 15-20 times in duels, explore all the moves and exits of Daeya, learn the secrets of instant transitions and get stuck in them countless times. His Adoleeseet friend Chapius will survey the entire depository of Adolees, and with each new discovery, he will resort to Davkaleon in order to check the next guess together. They will survive jointly by a miracle; however, they will never get to Twierks."

"I see there's no reason to show you this part," Ecktoral smiled. "You have guessed it all."

"Okay, show me Davkaleon in - let us say three years."
Ecktoral nodded.

The image on the wall screen changed. A tall, sturdy guy looked into the distance. He resembled Davkaleon but looked significantly older. His muscles, already impressive when he was younger, are rock hard.

"Look," said Ecktoral. *"He will soon be 18. In a couple of months, he will finish his military school. By Daeyan standards, he is already an adult man."*

"And is he still interested in Heather?" clarified Adamant.

"Yes. My mage Eximi regularly arranges meetings for him with her. True, very short meetings, but memorable, with enough adrenaline in the blood." He laughed.

Chapter 7. Interrupted Dream

Davkaleon sat on a highchair resembling a throne. In the spacious hall before him, girls danced. He was captivated by a beautiful dancer with golden hair, and he nodded his head in her direction. The girl moved towards an elegant dais where several other contenders for the attention of the supreme commander of the Daeya's army sat. The remaining girls continued to dance. Someone unnoticed approached the chair from behind and began to rock it. While still watching the dancers, Davkaleon swung at the one who dared to distract him from the pleasant spectacle. It didn't help. The chair shook even more. Jumping to his feet, Davkaleon grabbed the intruder.

Why are you fighting?" a familiar voice echoed. Davkaleon rubbed his eyes. The throne-like chair, the spacious hall, and most importantly, the girls, had disappeared. He was on the bed in his room. In the corner, his friend from Adolees was rubbing a bruise.

"Davkaleon, when you sleep, your temper gets out of hand," complained the teenager.

"Chapius, is that you? What are you doing here? Interrupting such a dream! Couldn't let me see it through to the end!" protested Davkaleon.

"You had such a blissful expression on your face, as if you had already become the supreme commander," Chapius laughed.

"Even better! In the dream, I already became a Commander, won several battles, and even received some awards. I picked the loveliest flowers, created the best flowerbed in Daeya. I was ready for the most enjoyable part, and then you showed up! You didn't let me finish the most exciting part!" sighed the disappointed would-be commander.

"Why do you need flowers?" Chapius didn't understand. "If you want flowers so much, next time I'll bring you a whole bouquet."

Davkaleon waved his hand dismissively.

"Chapius, these are not just flowers. In Daeya, *flowers* refer to girls, mind you - beautiful girls. What marvelous dolls I chose for myself! And then, instead of dolls - there you were."

"Let's watch your dream together," Chapius suggested. "If you've chosen enough of these dolls, there should be some left for me, too."

"As if I'd let anyone into my mind," Davkaleon cut him off. "Get to the point. Where do you want to drag me this time?"

Since their first encounter, the appearance of Chapa-Chapius-ChapiusKloyAlfreiDon meant another adventure, and usually a dangerous one. Davkaleon didn't object to this part—he enjoyed it.

"I need to go to the DRAGON corridor," Chapius cheerfully replied.

"I wouldn't mind a trip to the DRAGON corridor either," Davkaleon grinned. "If only you could tell me how to get there, you'd be priceless."

"I'll tell you!" Chapius's eyes gleamed with joy. "You can access the DRAGON corridor from the Mage's Chamber!"

"Chapius, we read about the fact that one can access

the DRAGON corridor from the Chamber of Mages in the manuscripts of the jeweler Pyromis three years ago! Do you have the slightest idea where to find this Chamber of Mages?"

"I do!" A joyful smile lit Chapius's face from ear to ear. The smile didn't last long. Sighing, Chapius added, "You see, it seems you can access the Chamber of Mages from the Pillantelli cave."

"So, can you or does it just seem so?" Davkaleon clarified, watching the disappearance of the smile from his friend's face.

"How should I know until I try?" Chapius replied. "Let's give it a shot, then we'll know."

"Let's give it a shot!" Davkaleon mocked. "Last time you tried with the temple in the rock, its owner nearly sent us to the shadow realm."

"Firstly, he didn't send us but just tattered slightly. And secondly, it's called a scientific experiment," Chapius replied nonchalantly.

"Alright, explain it properly," demanded Davkaleon.

"You see, I think I've figured out the DRAGON's numbering system!" declared Chapius. His eyes sparkled again; he was clearly proud of himself. "But I need to double-check it," Chapius added, sounding a bit sad.

"And you think that's a good explanation?" Davkaleon chuckled.

"Didn't I tell you that 666 is the DRAGON's favorite number?" Chapius inquired, as if that explained everything. "No one in Adolees is allowed to use this number for anything. There's no house with that number on any street," Chapius continued to explain.

"And what does that have to do with anything?" Davkaleon impatiently asked.

"The depository doesn't explain which number to use for the transition from the Mage's Chamber to the DRAGON corridor, but I'm sure it's the number 666. However, in the Mage's Base-12 numeral system, the DRAGON's number 666 becomes the mage's number 777. So, we probably should use 777 instead of 666. I don't know which one. Let's go and try!"

"Hold on a second, don't rush," demanded Davkaleon, in whose mind a vague guess flickered at the mention of the numerical system. "Do you think the small chambers at the end of the corridors in the Pillantelli cave are the Mage's Chambers?"

"Not all the corridors, just one, and not the chamber from which you took the jeweler's notes, but the one you can access from that chamber," Chapius corrected, adding, "At least, that's what I understood when I read the explanation in the Adolees Depository."

"You mean the corridor with the code in base-12 system?" clarified Davkaleon.

"Not exactly," disagreed Chapius. "Many can enter that corridor, but I believe that only someone with the blood of mages can access the Mage's Chamber and move from there to the DRAGON corridor. And from the DRAGON corridor, we can get to the Dragon-net, at least, that's how it seems to me," Davkaleon made an impatient gesture, urging Chapius to get to the point. Why did he need to go to the Dragon-net?

"Davkaleon, you're acting strange. Even during our first meeting when I told you about the DRAGON of Adolees, you dreamed of becoming the supreme commander of Daeya, while I become the DRAGON of Adolees. And now, when I'm trying to make it happen, you're not satisfied!"

"You told me that to become the DRAGON of Adolees, one must kill the DRAGON of Adolees! Is that what you're planning to do? Right now? Don't you think you should grow up a bit first? Do you remember your DRAGON? He is three times longer and five times thicker than you! How do you plan to fight him? Even if I help you, he will eat both of us, after roasting us first. Postpone the battle with the DRAGON for a few years. Then I'll be the first to wish you victory and, by the way, place my bet on you. Don't forget to let me know when this significant event is approaching. I'll settle all my debts. Just don't dare to lose!"

"Davkaleon, I can't postpone the meeting with the DRAGON of Adolees for a few years," sighed Chapius, "if I do that, I won't become the great DRAGON of Adolees."

"Why?" Davkaleon's patience was clearly running thin.

"I've seen something that cannot be, at least, it *shouldn't be*," Chapius sadly replied. "But I know that in Adolees, a fight for a duel with the great DRAGON is about to begin. And if a new great DRAGON appears, young and strong, I won't be able to defeat him in the near future."

"Do you think you can defeat the current DRAGON? Right now?" Davkaleon pointedly twirled his finger at his temple.

"Not right now. But I want to try to persuade the DRAGON to set a date for the duel in advance, and to do so now. You see, in Adolees, it's believed that if a new great DRAGON appears on Dragon Day, it brings luck and prosperity. In four years, there will be the three thousandth anniversary of the first DRAGON's appearance. If we schedule the duel on that day, the winner will be surrounded by an aura of good fortune. It's such a sacred date for all of Adolees that anyone attempting to force a duel with the DRAGON before that day, after the announcement of this date, will be considered the ultimate traitor of Adolees. I want to try to negotiate with the DRAGON to set the duel on the anniversary day. I'll have four years to grow," Chapius smiled.

"Why do you think your DRAGON would agree to that? What's in it for him?" Davkaleon wondered.

"In Adolees, they believe that the Great DRAGON, despite his imperiousness and cruelty, is devoted to Adolees and cares for it. That's what I'm counting on," Chapius replied.

"Let's suppose you're right," Davkaleon said. "Your DRAGON is indeed so devoted to Adolees that he values it more than his own life, and he's even willing to part with his ephemeral existence for the happiness of the Adoleeseets. Explain to me, what benefit does Adolees gain from having another DRAGON instead of the current one? And why is this benefit so obvious that your DRAGON will listen to you with gratitude, agree with you without objection, and release us from his Dragon-net without having us for lunch?"

"The moment of the meeting will be the most challenging," sighed Chapius. "If the DRAGON gets enraged, he'll swallow us before I even start speaking. I need to figure out how to distract him for at least a few seconds, and then my eloquence will convince him that I'm right."

"Your eloquence?" Davkaleon laughed. "You've been explaining to me for a whole 15 minutes and still haven't gotten to the point of why your DRAGON would even engage in a duel with someone."

And Chapius explained that the DRAGON is about to turn 300 years old."

"That much?" Davkaleon was surprised.

"Yes, don't interrupt me," Chapius insisted before continuing his story. "Fire-breathing Dragons live long lives, but even they don't always survive their 150th anniversary, and if they do, they weaken. The new DRAGON is always the strongest. It's not surprising that the strongest, upon becoming the DRAGON, lives longer than ordinary dragons, but even for him, reaching the age of 300 is a lot. As long as the DRAGON is full of strength, no one even dares to think about fighting with him. He can easily handle anyone with playful ease. But the age of 300 changes everything. In a week, the entire Adolees will be celebrating Dragon Day."

A few days earlier, Chapius, as a student at the Fire-Breathing Dragon school, attended a training session conducted by the great DRAGON himself. Before the training, the students were responsible for tidying up. It was a common practice; after all, fighting Dragons wouldn't bother with such nonsense. It was Chapius's turn to clean last time. He cleaned everywhere it was required, even entered the guild of fire-breathing Dragons, and approached the lodge of the DRAGON. On one hand, it wasn't allowed, but on the other hand, someone had to clean there. Chapius wanted to finish cleaning before the DRAGON arrived, but this time the DRAGON came earlier than usual and Chapius didn't manage to disappear.

"You?! How dare you loiter here?!" roared the DRAGON and took a step towards Chapius.

Chapius rushed towards the exit, and the DRAGON lunged after him. In the path of the DRAGON lay a broom that Chapius used for cleaning, and the DRAGON stumbled over it. Chapius froze. It couldn't be! It was all in his imagination! A stumbling DRAGON?! It was like saying it's bright at night and dark during the day! It meant admitting that Adolees was weak and helpless. Since ancient times, the great DRAGON symbolized the strength of Adolees. If there were enemies on his way, he would annihilate them. If there were obstacles, he would destroy them. If the DRAGON stumbled, it meant he had weakened; he could no longer defend Adolees. It meant the time had come for the Great Battle and a New DRAGON.

Chapius knew that if the DRAGON wanted to kill him, running would be futile. The DRAGON would catch him in two leaps. The DRAGON stood motionless, as if he himself was struck by what had happened. Chapius stood still, not breathing.

"Come here," growled the DRAGON as he moved back to his lodge-seat.

Chapius approached, neither alive nor dead. The DRAGON took out a large bottle of the Drink of Power and took a sip.

"How many times have you annoyed me?" asked the DRAGON, examining Chapius. "First with your name, then you dared to call yourself my apprentice along with your Daeyan, then with stealing records from the temple. And last time — what did you forget in the Pillantelli cave?"

"I..." Chapius began, trying to come up with a better explanation for the reason behind his search for the Gates of the End.

The DRAGON waved his paw, indicating that he wasn't interested in Chapius's answer, and took a few more sips of his drink.

"You befriended your Daeyan, but Daeya and Adolees are enemies. They're not on the same path. What will you do if you meet him on the battlefield?" the DRAGON asked, studying Chapius.

"I'll try to resolve disagreements peacefully, but if that's not possible, I'll defend Adolees," Chapius firmly replied.

Upon hearing these words, the DRAGON burst into laughter.

"Resolve disagreements peacefully!" the DRAGON repeated Chapius's words several times. "Since when do Adolees's Dragons resolve disagreements peacefully?" After calming down, the DRAGON hissed, "Forget what you saw, or I'll kill you!" and added very quietly, "If you're so insistently intruding into the Pillantelli cave, at least figure out the corridors and their counting systems."

After training, Chapius headed to the Depository to figure out what the DRAGON had pointed him to. He was near one of the shelves when he overheard a conversation between two fire-breathing Dragons.

"Are you sure we don't need the approval of the Fire-Breathers Guild to declare a battle?" one Dragon asked.

Chapius realized that someone else, besides him, had witnessed the DRAGON stumbling. He froze by the shelf, listening to the conversation. The Dragons were reading the rules. From what Chapius understood, any Dragon could initiate a battle with the DRAGON at any time on their own initiative, and approval from the Fire-Breathers Guild was not required for that. However, this rule applied only if the initiator of the battle was not the DRAGON himself. Otherwise, the battle had to follow completely different rules. Participants had to announce their participation in advance to the Fire-Breathers Guild and undergo preliminary fights. The winner of the final battle immediately entered into combat with the Great DRAGON. There was no time for rest. In this battle, either he perished, or bells rang throughout Adolees, and in the Guild of Fire-Breathers Dragons, the phrase echoed, "The Great DRAGON of Adolees has died. Long live the Great DRAGON of Adolees."

"The Great DRAGON always knows what's happening in Adolees. If I know that Dragons are preparing for the battle, then he surely knows about it," Chapius concluded his story.

"And do you think the DRAGON will agree to declare a battle that will take place in four years? Do your rules allow postponing a battle for such an extended period?" asked Davkaleon.

"The rules don't specify a timeframe," replied Chapius, "but, as I mentioned, a three-thousand-year anniversary is worth waiting four years for. In Adolees, everyone will applaud such a decision of the DRAGON, and he knows it."

"You say that only those with the blood of mages can enter the Mage's Chamber. We can't boast about the blood of mages, but we have the Neophyte Rings. Maybe they will help us," noted Davkaleon.

"I thought about that," sighed Chapius, "but we have just crawled onto the third level. Clearly, that's not enough to pass as mages."

"The third level is certainly not enough, but if we add the mage potion to it, it might just work," Davkaleon elaborated his idea.

"Exactly! That's exactly what I wanted to suggest! Did I forget to mention that to you?" Chapius rejoiced at Davkaleon's insight.

"You say that the DRAGON's number 666 transforms into the mages' number 777. Do you mean that it's the same number written in different number systems?" asked Davkaleon.

"Yes. Mages use a base-12 system, while the DRAGON uses a base-13 system. The DRAGON's system is unique. When converting from the DRAGON's system to another system, you need to first subtract or add the difference between these systems, and then convert the number itself," Chapius tried to explain.

"Alright, Chapius, I will go with you to the Pillantelli cave, and from there to the Mage's Chamber and the Dragon-net to your DRAGON," said Davkaleon, "but you'll have to prepare the mage potion yourself. We are taught ethics and some other nonsense lessons at school."

"What lessons?" Chapius asked, surprised. "Today is a Sunday. I intentionally arrived at your place early so you wouldn't disappear anywhere."

"Don't rub salt in my wounds," sighed Davkaleon. "Do you think I wanted this? Like I went to the school bosses and volunteered for these lessons because without the knowledge of how to bow to whom, which foot to put forward, and all the other nonsense, I can't survive. But the bosses believe that graduates of the military school should know how to pretend to be polite goody-goody, and they found no other time in the schedule to fit these lessons. Peach Ball is coming soon, and they've decided to take away our weekends. Today will be the first lesson. They'll be showing us how not to step on girls' toes during dances and telling us not to gaze at another girl while dancing with the first. As if I didn't know that already!"

"What is the Peach Ball?" asked Chapius.

"Peaches, flowers, dolls, girls, brides," Davkaleon listed the names the Daeyans used for the ball. "Call it what you want. It's the place where they try to marry you off, and the flowers hide their thorns and save them for later."

"But you said that marrying before the graduation

night is forbidden at your school," Chapius remarked.

"Well, there are a couple of months left until graduation night. The Brides' Ball is in a month. Just enough time to instill in us the idea that a married officer advances in his career faster. You should have heard how they tried to convince us that practicing dances and refining bows on weekends is fun," Davkaleon explained.

"Why do your school bosses want you to get married?" Chapius wondered.

"Why? Do you know what kind of business it is?" Davkaleon waved his hand toward Chapius. "How could you know, with Adolees having the custom of having only one wife! In Daeya, you could say the whole economy relies on this. You have to pay a ransom for the bride."

"Ransom?" surprised Chapius.

"Ransom, bride dowry, bride price, call it as you want. It is money paid by a groom or his family to the girl-bride. The more beautiful the girl, the higher the ransom. And if the girl is from a good family, educated, and well-groomed, the price goes through the roof. For money matters, they turn to the bank. Do you think the school would miss such an opportunity? No way! For every bank loan taken by a graduate, there are commissions. So, the school is interested in cramming 3-4 wives onto each graduate. At the same time, our kind mentors and commanders solve their financial problems. Each of them has several daughters, for whom you can get good money. That's why they tell us that if you're not married, don't count on a good position."

"Is that really what they say?" asked Chapius.

"Not exactly, but close. Like, who would trust command to a person with neither a wife nor children? Well, you prepare the potion for now, and I'll tidy myself up and go study etiquette with Mr. Pusik. And where did they manage to find a teacher with that name?" Davkaleon said, heading towards the door.

*****

"Keep in mind, all women are witches. Even the most well-behaved ones are still witches. There are no non-witches. If you think you found a non-witch, it means she's the worst kind of witch because she knows how to pretend," declared the little bald Mr. Pusik.

"Two brides ran away from him from a wedding, and he won't calm down," someone whispered from behind.

"That's slander! Not two, but one!" protested Mr. Pusik. "And not from the wedding, but during the bride's viewing, and she didn't run away, I just didn't want to marry her."

A few giggles echoed in the class. Mr. Pusik stomped his feet and let out a shrill scream, "If you don't stop right now, we'll be here until evening."

The laughter instantly died down. No one wanted to sit there until evening. Mr. Pusik then continued to develop the topic.

"Remember, there's nothing worse than a scholarly witch. An unschooled one might not be so guilty of being born a witch, for she didn't have a choice. But a scholarly witch knew exactly why she was studying. To become a witch! If you encounter one, run away, don't even think about marrying her, or you'll ruin your entire life. Know this, all troubles stem from science. If there were no scholars, Daeya would flourish. And from witchy science, double troubles arise."

For the next half hour, Mr. Pusik continued to scare the class with tales of witches and their tricks.

"So, what should we do if everyone around is a witch?" someone from the students asked.

"Unfortunately, even the best Daeyans can't do anything about it. It would be best not to get involved with witches, but that's not Daeya's way at all," sighed Pusik. "Daeya needs children, and children don't just appear on their own; they need a family. I'm here to prepare you for the inevitable difficulties you'll face at the upcoming ball."

It turns out, Mr. Pusik also knew how to dance. However, the male population of Daeya could learn to dance in 15 minutes. All that was required of them was to offer the lady either their right or left hand and occasionally express profound admiration with nods of their heads. The ladies were taught to flutter around their partners and perform incredible dance moves. But even these simple requirements applied only to official balls; the rest of the time, the male population of Daeya preferred to be spectators.

Chapter 8. Traveling to the Mages' Chamber

"Finally, we're here! Davkaleon! You've gotten so heavy, my back hurts," complained Chapius as he landed in Pillantelli's cave.

"Where are you going?" Aleurh said.

"Aleurh?!" Davkaleon and Chapius were surprised. "How did you know we were heading for the cave?"

"I saw Elfid come to visit. Nine times out of ten, that means Chapius has taken on the appearance of Elfid. I waited for you to come and get me, but you never did," Aleurh replied testily.

"Aleurh, I'm not sure you can get in where we want you to go. I'm not even sure we can get in there ourselves," Davkaleon began to explain.

"What kind of secret place is it that a Daeyan dragon can't get in?" Aleurh raged.

"Do you remember our first flight to the temple in the rock, when Chapa and I took the mage potion? You couldn't enter the temple then either," Davkaleon asked.

"So what? I was right there in the middle of it. Interesting! And how we fought afterwards! It's still a joy to remember!"

They explained and even apologized for a long time before the offended Aleurh calmed down. Chapius had to repeat everything he had already told Davkaleon.

"Why not go straight into the corridor with numbering system base13?" Aleurh asked. "Last time you said something about the DRAGON system and said that it was connected with the number 13."

71

"That's because the Mages' Chamber should be entered from the Mages' Corridor. At least that's what I understood," Chapius explained.

"All right, if that's the way it is, let's go," Aleurh said, clearly done with the argument.

"Wait a minute. Before we go in, we need to drink the mage potion," Davkaleon said.

"We've gotten older, so I thought we should have more of this potion," said Chapius, handing Davkaleon a decent sized bottle.

"Do you think this is the right amount?" Davkaleon asked doubtfully, remembering that four years earlier, when he had first taken the mages' drink, it had only been a small flask.

"Of course!" Chapius replied with great conviction. "Don't hesitate. If you need more, I have more. I've made plenty." Chapius proudly showed a few more bottles.

"I actually thought that was too much, but all right," Davkaleon agreed and drained the whole bottle. His head rumbled.

"Perhaps that was too much," Davkaleon suggested.

"How about another one?" Chapius asked.

Instead of answering, Davkaleon stepped into the corridor. Chapius and Aleurh followed him. After walking down the corridor, they found themselves at a dead end. There was a small ledge on one of the walls. Davkaleon pricked himself with his dagger. A drop of blood fell on the ledge and an image of a palm appeared on it. Before placing his hand with Neophyte's ring, Davkaleon drained another bottle of potion in a volley. Chapius did the same.

Everything flickered and swirled before their eyes. The Chamber of Mages apparently did not like Neophyte's ring.

"What?! Those are Neophyte rings! Imposters! Cheeky Impudents! Liars! Upstarts! You dare come in here without the Mage's ring!"

The wall with the ledge disappeared, but the three eager to enter the Chamber of Mages were not happy about it. A fire raged ahead. Davkaleon took a step back and froze, feeling the heat. Flames raged behind him as well. Dragons are not afraid of fire, at least not if you don't stay in it too long, and Chapius, without thinking, immediately turned into a dragon. Davkaleon had no such luxury. Worst of all, the fire was slowly but steadily approaching the sspot where Davkaleon stood.

*****

"Let them pass. Let them through!" Adamant demanded. "Have your mage quickly prepare a puzzle they can solve. I want to see if they can think under stress."

"They're used to stress," Ecktoral said.

"They're used to fighting under stress, and I want to see if they can think under stress," Adamant replied.

"Eximi!" Ecktoral called out.

Fire surrounded Davkaleon on all sides.

"I can lift you up," Aleurh growled, looking around.

"I don't think that would do any good," Davkaleon replied. "You'd better see if there's something lurking behind the fire."

"Yes! Hiding! Look!" Chapius shouted. Behind the flames, indeed, there was a panel of sorts.

"There's a series of numbers from 0 to 9," added Chapius. "And they can be pressed."

"Then press it! You said 777 was the number of mages. Then that's what we need!"

Alas, the fire soared to the ceiling and came even closer.

"Try 666," Davkaleon shouted. "Since that's your DRAGON's favorite number, he might like it, and we'll end up in the DRAGON's corridor."

It seems 666 was the right answer, because the fire retreated. Unfortunately, it didn't disappear completely; it just made it possible to get closer to the panel with the numbers. The row of numbers from 0 to 9 wasn't the only one. Just behind it, some sort of inscription could be seen. It seemed to be a mixture of numbers and letters. The fire surrounding it made it impossible to see the inscription more closely. Chapius rushed forward, and was immediately thrown back.

"Wow!" He was outraged, rubbing a bruised spot on his arm.

Aleurh moved toward the inscription, but was thrown back, too. Aleurh jumped up to throw himself at the invisible barrier, but Chapius stopped him.

"Come on, that won't help. We need to guess what the text is."

All three of them looked around for a clue. A crystal ball hung from the ceiling. The glow of fire danced on its edges. And there was a reflection of an inscription hidden by the fire.

"We have to guess what X equals," said Chapius, and then he stopped talking.

"Elfid should be here," sighed Davkaleon.

"Maybe so. The sum of the two end digits is 9, because 8 and 1 is 9. The sum of the two previous digits is 7 because 2 and 5 is 7. That's 2 less than 9. So, the next sum must be 2 less than 7. Therefore, X equals 5," Chapius suggested.

Davkaleon was not impressed by this suggestion. Aleurh tried to grasp the meaning of what Chapius said.

"Where did you see the last two digits if there's only one X?" Aleurh asked.

Chapius did not answer. He already had another idea. Meanwhile, the fire was getting worse.

"Wait, wait," Davkaleon tried to negotiate with the fire. "We guessed 666, we'll guess this time too."

"How long should I wait?" growled an invisible voice. "Idiots!"

"The crystal ball is like a mirror" Davkaleon realized. "Elfid had once shown me magic tricks with mirrors. What is actually on the right side will be on the left in the mirror, and vice versa. So, the real inscription is not '8 2 X 5 1', but '1 5 X 2 8'."

"If this is true, then notice how the numbers are written. For 8, 1, and X, it doesn't matter whether you look at them from right to left or vice versa. For 2 and 5, it makes a difference. They should change, too," Chapius pointed out.

"Let's check it out," suggested Davkaleon.

Fortunately, Davkaleon's pockets were filled with various items, including parchment. Davkaleon copied the writing in the crystal ball onto a piece of parchment. Aleurh reached up and brought the note closer to the crystal ball, and they could clearly see the original writing.

"I know what it is!" rejoiced Chapius. "In our school they call it the sequence of life. This is only a small part of the sequence. It starts as 1, 1, 2, 3, 5, 8, 13."

"You can tell us later," Davkaleon cut him off. "Tell me, what is X equal to?"

"X equals 3," replied Chapius in an aggrieved voice.

"If you are sure that X equals 3, then press 3, and see what happens." Aleurh suggested.

"Finally, at least you've figured out how to cheat!" said the disgruntled voice.

"Are you going to let us through?" Davkaleon asked.

"I'm considering whether we need crooks in the DRAGON corridor," replied the voice.

Soon, the verdict was announced: "Okay, come on in."

A passage opened up ahead. It appeared to be a DRAGON corridor. Chapius, Davkaleon, and Aleurh entered the passage. As they walked down the passage, they looked with interest at the drawings glorifying the strength and power of dragons. There were many dragons, and they were all different. For the first few minutes, nothing happened. Then the lights in the corridor went out, and the floor ripped forward. Davkaleon, Chapius, and Aleurh rushed among glowing skeletons, voracious sharks, and fire-breathing dragons. They felt water pouring, fire burning, and wind whistling. Monster paws and monster faces reached out to them. After circling the labyrinths for a few minutes, the floor slowed. A light glimmered ahead. Some kind of monster jumped out of the wall. Aleurh struck it with a paw and froze - the paw went through the air. After navigating the labyrinth and enduring attacks from skeletons with clattering teeth, they finally reached a narrow passage.

The wall of water in the passage appeared suddenly. Chapius, Davkaleon, and Aleurh froze in front of it, unable to believe their eyes. Water would typically spill over, right? This water did not spill; it stood upright, filling the hallway from floor to ceiling. Chapius, Davkaleon and Aleurh even touched it to make sure it was indeed the liquid that splashes in the ocean and pours when it rains.

"Would you like to wait for me here?" Chapius has offered. "I'll grow gills in no time, so water won't be a problem for me. I'll find the DRAGON, and then I'll come back to you."

Davkaleon and Aleurh had no time to reply. Either they were thrown forward or the wall of water came toward them, but the water came in waves and swept them away. The current swept them forward with such force that Davkaleon began to fear that it would carry them into Tartar. It was a good guess—the jeweler's manuscripts said that the Dragon's corridor could be accessed from it.

After a few minutes, Davkaleon stopped worrying about Tartar and wondered how much air he would have before he suffocated. They stopped abruptly. Davkaleon felt the current continue to carry on at the same speed, but he himself and Chapius and Aleurh stayed in one place and froze in front of a sign on the wall. It was the Sign of the DRAGON. Chapius touched it, and Davkaleon and Chapius found themselves in a magnificent hall. But Aleurh wasn't around. He was probably still floundering in the water. Though alarmed, Davkaleon did not panic—dragons could go without air for much longer than the Daeyans.

"What are you doing here?" The DRAGON roared, staring at Chapius. The huge dragon sprawled in the dragon bed. He paid no attention to Davkaleon for the time being.

"The Great DRAGON of Adolees ..." Chapius began his prepared speech.

"Anyway," the DRAGON yawned and, glancing toward Davkaleon, added, "it's good that you thought to bring me lunch. I can see you're starting to think."

"No, no, he's not for lunch," Chapius grumbled.

Davkaleon realized he had to intervene. "Postpone the fight for four years," he said.

"What?!" jumped the DRAGON. "You, miserable lizard! How dare you blabber about our customs!" The DRACON grabbed Chapius with two fingers of his huge paw and opened his fearsome mouth.

"Leave ChapiusCloyAlfreyDon alone. You kept his name for a reason. You knew he would make a great new Great DRAGON of Adolees, so why alter your plans?" Davkaleon continued talking as if nothing had happened.

The DRAGON's eyes filled with blood. Throwing Chapius aside, he turned to Davkaleon.

"Daeyan, last time I warned you that our next meeting would be our last. This meeting has come to an end." The DRAGON rose to his full height.

"I remember," Davkaleon quickly agreed, "but you

didn't say you were going to turn me into a steak then. So, why don't we have a friendly chat the last time we met?

"Friendly?" DRAGON grinned.

"Of course! Chapius is offering you the chance to become a legend! In your Adolees, they still celebrate the day the first DRAGON appeared. All other DRACONs are repeats of the first one. Even the name is the same. Can you tell me the names of those who became DRAGONs after the first one? I don't mean ChapiusCloyAlfreyDon. That name is obvious. How about the names that the DRAGONs had before they became Great DRAGONs? Do you remember them yourself?

"Davkaleon, that's not customary in Adolees," was the startled voice of Chapius.

"You'd be surprised, but I remember them all," replied the DRAGON, looking at Davkaleon thoughtfully.

Davkaleon didn't like something in that answer, but he couldn't figure out what it was. The DRAGON had changed his mind about turning him into an appetizer, at least immediately, so what more could he want?

"Great DRAGON," Chapius rumbled, "if you set the fight for the three-thousandth anniversary of Dragon Day, all of Adolees will applaud your decision. It's such a sacred date for all of Adolees that the winner will be enveloped in an aura of good fortune. And you will be remembered as the greatest of the Great DRAGONs who brought happiness to all of Adolees. You will be called the Great 13th! There will be monuments to you all over Adolees!"

"Shut up," the DRAGON said. "What you're saying is obvious."

"So, you agree?" Chapius asked.

"You are dreaming that this miserable lizard," the DRAGON nodded at Chapius, "will become the DRAGON of Adolees and dance to your tune."

"No!" said Davkaleon. "I will not interfere in Adolees' affairs. Why should I? I have my Daeya. That's all I need!"

"That's why you've been inciting since the first time you and he met." The DRAGON nodded his head, and a scene of Davkaleon talking to little Chapa-Chapius appeared in the air.

"And your parents chose the name of DRAGON for you!" smiled Davkaleon. "So now, you are obligated to become a DRAGON! You must be a fire-breathing one—otherwise, they wouldn't give you such name. So, the only thing you need to do is to kill a present DRAGON. The Gods knew what they were doing when they brought us together! I will go to a military school. When I grow up, I will become the Commander of Daeya's Army. Imagine how great we will be! You will be the DRAGON of Adolees. I will be the Commander of Daeya! Together, we will defeat any enemies!" There was not the slight shadow of doubt in Davkaleon's voice that this was their future.

"And what's wrong with that?" Davkaleon objected. "Where did I say anything about dictating to Chapius what he should do?"

"Yeah, well, a little thing like killing me doesn't count," the DRAGON said, grinning.

"It's in your tradition," Davkaleon said. "If you're going to have a fight anyway, don't you care who it's with?"

82

"You knew nothing of our traditions at the time, but the life of the Lord of Adolees meant less than nothing to you. And it means nothing to you now. And neither does Adolees himself, along with all the Adoleeseets."

"Of all the Adoleeseets, I know only Chapius, and as you may have noticed, he has seen only good things from me," Davkaleon objected.

"I can see that you two have become friends. That's the problem. Daeya and Adolees are enemies. They can't be together. What will you do when you meet on the battlefield? Will you declare your love for each other and swear eternal friendship?" The DRAGON asked mockingly and added, "Oh, yes, how did I forget? You will try to resolve your differences peacefully."

"Why can't we settle our differences peacefully? What's wrong with that?" Davkaleon asked.

"Nothing," replied the DRACON, "except that Adolees and Daeya cannot enter the Gates of the End together."

Davkaleon remembered the argument with Chapius about the Gates of the End and the journey to Pillantelli's cave.

"All right, the Gates of the End are not relevant yet," the DRACON said in a peaceful manner, "are you really attached to that pathetic creature?" He asked Davkaleon, nodding at Chapius.

"He's not pathetic at all!" Davkaleon said indignantly. "He's just a child!"

"A child who dreams of taking my place," the DRAGON grinned. "Do you realize that even after four years I can handle him with one paw?"

"You can, but you can train him," said Davkaleon in a sneaky voice.

"Train him?! So he can kill me?"

"I didn't invent your customs," Davkaleon said. "As far as I'm concerned, if you don't declare a fight, they'll declare a fight for you."

"I can win," said the DRAGON.

"You can," Davkaleon didn't argue. "But in the end, you will lose. So why don't you go so that you'll be the stuff of legends?"

"Who cares about your legends," said the DRAGON. "Listen attentively! Only those who have DRAGON's blood in them can defeat a DRAGON, at least that was the case with the twelve who ruled Adolees after the first one." The DRAGON grinned.

"They were apprentices of the DRAGON!" Chapius guessed. "All of them! Including you!"

"That's right," replied the DRAGON.

"Then make him your apprentice!" Davkaleon exclaimed.

"No DRAGON has ever taken on an apprentice for his beautiful eyes," the DRAGON grinned.

"What do you want for it?" Davkaleon asked.

"It's going to cost you a lot," the DRAGON squinted his eyes.

"Me? Why me?" Davkaleon wondered.

"And who? Him? You claim he's a child."

"I am *not* a child! I can take responsibility for myself," Chapius was indignant.

"Shut up," the DRAGON shrugged him off.

"How much do you want?" Davkaleon asked.

"Do you think we're talking about money?" DRAGON grinned. "Money won't help. If you want me to take him on as an apprentice, I need real payment. You can give me your Aleurh."

"No!!!" Davkaleon cried out in horror.

"Why not? He'll soon suffocate in the water anyway," the DRAGON remarked.

"Dragons can go without air for a long time," Davkaleon said.

"They can, but not indefinitely. How long have we been talking?"

"Don't take Aleurh away from me!!! Give me a different price!"

"Well, a different one, then. I'm being kind today. We spoke today about the Gates of the End. I need you to go there."

"All right! When? Now?" Davkaleon asked.

"No. There's no need for that now. You will go there during the battle of the candidates for my place. If you try to sneak out, that little brat won't live to fight me," the DRAGON nodded at Chapius. "In the Gates of the End you will find the Black Rose - Dragon Power Amulet. And he will win all the qualifying fights."

"How do I enter the Gates of the End and what do I have to do with this Amulet?" Davkaleon asked.

"I'll make you a tattoo. It will allow you to enter the Gates of the End from the DRAGON corridor. As for the Amulet, hold it to the tattoo and it will tell you what to do."

"How do I get back from the Gates of the End?" Davkaleon asked.

"Simple," the DRAGON grinned. "After the battle, the great DRAGON will be your Adoleeseet friend. He will bring you back."

"Davkaleon, I swear you won't be alone there for long. I'll join you right after the battle and we'll explore all around. I'll be the Great DRAGON at that time, so nothing bad will happen to you!" exclaimed Chapius.

"And you're asking me to make this miserable lizard my apprentice?" laughed the DRAGON.

Davkaleon hesitated. On the one hand, things were looking good. If DRAGON would take Chapius as his apprentice, little Adoleeseet would have a chance to win the fight. But why did Davkaleon have a feeling that something wasn't right here?

"Keep in mind; this isn't just about whether or not I take him on as an apprentice. Your answer will determine your Aleurh's life and yours as well," the DRAGON grinned.

"Let Aleurh in here. I agree," Davkaleon answered.

"I'll let him in after the tattoo. On which shoulder do you prefer the decoration?" DRAGON asked.

"On any shoulder," Davkaleon said.

"Drink!" the DRAGON demanded and held out a goblet of sizzling liquid.

"Am I a delicate young girl who can't handle a tattoo without your drink?" Davkaleon asked indignantly.

"You can't handle my tattoo without this drink. Drink! It's part of the ritual."

Davkaleon drained the goblet in a gulp. His head rumbled. He saw and felt the rest as if in a dream. The DRAGON seemed to sink its teeth into his shoulder. A searing pain pierced his entire body. Blood dripped from the DRAGON's mouth. Maybe it was just Davkaleon's imagination.

"Drink!" he heard the DRAGON shout.

"I've already drunk it," replied Davkaleon.

"This is a different drink. The one you drank before the tattoo, and this one you must drink after."

Davkaleon drained the cup. His head cleared. His shoulder still stung, but it was tolerable.

"Now let Aleurh in," he demanded.

"I already did," the DRAGON shrugged.

"My friend," said Davkaleon to Aleurh, "we're going to get out of here."

"You will, but not right away. You'll have my treats before you do," said the DRAGON.

As if by magic, tables with food and drinks appeared in the hall. Who would have thought that a conversation with Adolees' DRAGON could take place without the threat of being turned into steak? The food was excellent, and the DRAGON even managed to pose as a gracious host.

"The Great DRAGON, if you write your biography, all Adoleeseets will ..." Chapius began.

"DRAGONS don't write memoirs," the DRAGON interrupted him.

"I mean write a biography before you became a DRAGON," Chapius persisted.

"There's no need for that. I have enough portraits," the DRAGON nodded at the wall.

There were portraits of thirteen DRAGONs in gorgeous gold frames. The portrait of the first DRAGON took up half of the wall; the others were smaller and on the other half. The thirteenth portrait was clearly the portrait of the current DRAGON.

"Why did the current DRAGON agree to have his portrait so small compared to the portrait of the first DRAGON?" A thought flashed through Davkaleon's mind. "Why did all the DRAGONs agree to this? Out of respect for the first one?"

"It's time to take care of the portrait of the next Great DRAGON of Adolees," said the DRAGON.

Another golden frame appeared on the wall. For now, it was empty.

"You'll look good here," the DRAGON said, looking at Chapius.

Somewhere far, far away in Davkaleon's subconscious mind, a hunch arose. A chill ran down his spine. He shifted his gaze from one portrait to another. Why did all the portraits seem alive to him? Maybe he'd had too many of the DRAGON's drinks. Neither Chapius nor Aleurh seemed to notice anything. Davkaleon shifted his gaze to the DRAGON. The DRACON in turn looked at him intently.

"The secrets of Dragon-net are unknown to anyone but the DRAGON. Nor will they be known to you," the DRAGON said in a cryptic voice.

"What secrets?"

A white mist filled the hall.

"Forget what you have seen," Davkaleon heard the DRAGON's voice. "Wipe it out of your memory, consign it to oblivion."

The voice of the DRACON grew quieter, the fog thickened. Davkaleon wanted to sleep. His eyes fell asleep. Sleep, sleep, *sleep*.

Chapter 9. "You Need a Girl"

Davkaleon opened his eyes and looked around. He was near the exit of the cave. His faithful dragon Aleurh was snoring peacefully beside him. A little farther away, Chapius was sleeping soundly. Davkaleon tried to rise, but his head was rumbling. He remembered the events that occurred after he entered the DRAGON Corridor with Chapius and Aleurh. Had it really happened, or had he dreamed it? He could find out. After all, the DRAGON had given him a tattoo. Where is it? Davkaleon glanced at his shoulder. Rose's drawing of a dragon caught his eye. So, what had happened was true.

Davkaleon looked out of the cave. He was on a mountainside in an unfamiliar place. But, what a place! It clearly wasn't Daeya. Such a fantastic place could only exist in a fairy tale. Just below was a flat area with a small silvery lake in the middle. Around the platform were mountains rising upwards, overgrown with unseen trees. It seemed as if several seasons were changing in a circle. Where Davkaleon was, it was most likely spring. The pleasant coolness of the breeze was refreshing. There was a spring near the cave, a babbling brook running down the slope. A little farther away, spring was changing into summer. Opposite, silver snowflakes swirled in the air. To the left, the golden and scarlet colors of autumn glowed. Below, the exuberant colors of summer played on the grounds. Trees stretched their branches toward each other and wove shady arbors. Fountains with iridescent jets could be seen between the trees. Rays from several suns shone through the trees.

Davkaleon heard a pleasant voice and immediately turned his head.

"Oh, Davkaleon! He's awake already! Girls, look how cute he is! And he's nobody's, at least for now! We can have fun!" Three young girls stood not far from the cave and made eyes at him.

"Lala, are you trying to sell him your witch potion? He won't fall for it."

"But he'll fall for the result," the one called Lala replied, and she ran her hands over her figure expressively.

Even if Lala, dressed in a shapeless sack, was standing without moving, it would be difficult not to pay attention to her figure. But Lala was not dressed in a shapeless rag. The dress was tight around her figure, and the length well above her knees caught Davkaleon's attention. Such outfits were not worn in Daeya. The girls were *clearly* not from Daeya. However, Davkaleon didn't care where they were from. The important thing was that they were here, and he liked them. *All of them.* If his mother had pointed a crossbow at him, and at the same time, in tears, began to reproach him for his heartless son wanting to leave her without grandchildren, he would have married them immediately. All of them! But there was no mom with a crossbow and tears, and there was no need to marry. That was even better.

"Lala, don't get yourself in trouble. Flower will be here in a minute. Mind you, she got herself a new broom yesterday. It's the latest model. Vertical lift. Load capacity - two Davkaleons," said the second girl.

"Why does she need two Davkaleons? Isn't one enough

for her?" asked the third girl, giving Davkaleon an appraising look.

"Why? Look, she herself, Davkaleon and his weapon. What if there's a coven on Ceres somewhere? You know what kind of coven they have there! But you can't go there unarmed," said the other girl.

"A coven?!" Davkaleon was surprised. The word was familiar, but Davkaleon tried to remember if he knew all the meanings of the word. Maybe it meant something else besides witches' gatherings? The girl dispelled his doubts. With a graceful wave of her hand, she sang:

> *Day and night there was a legion of Twierks witches and magicians at the miracle Twierks coven.*

"Tiger, don't scare us with Flower. We're all flowers. Aren't we, Aconite?" Lala grinned and winked at the other girl. "As for Flower, she's not coming, not even on her new broom. They haven't met yet. By the way, what model of broom did she buy? I offered her a great broom yesterday, even promised to split the commission with her. Keep in mind, if anyone needs a new broom, on my page in Witch-net, a full description with a hologram, demonstration, and ten-minute materialization. Have you seen anyone on the Witch-net offer a ten-minute materialization? Ha! Two minutes tops! And I've offered ten minutes! In that time, you can fly, try all the controls, and even adjust your seat. And if someone doesn't have enough money, I can arrange a witch's loan in a jiffy. And I'll split the commission in half. You know, always do!"

"Yes! You'll split the commission for the broom in half, but you'll forget about the commission for the insurance, and it's three times as much," Aconite grinned.

"No way!" Lala was indignant at this accusation. "I'm an honest witch. Ask anyone on the Witch-net, they'll all confirm it. If I say that the commission is half, then it is half. All of it! On the broom, on the loan, on the insurance and on the maintenance!"

"Are you not afraid that in 10 minutes on a decent broom it is possible, you know how far to fly?" Tiger was surprised. "And who will pay for fuel? You?"

"What fuel?! Do you really think I'm going to sell antediluvian models? My brooms fly only on clean power!" the pride for her goods clearly heard in Lala's voice.

"Especially on clean power! In 10 minutes, it is possible to fly far, far away, at the same time take the liked artifact, and, notice, not to pay for it. Who will bear the costs? You! Because the broom is yours!" Tiger insisted.

"No, not me. The insurance company. Before signing the contract, I showed it to the lawyers of the Witch-net. They confirmed that I did not risk anything. And as for the insurers from *A and Z*, behind them such forces that they will return what they pay. Not to mention that the price for their insurance is crazy."

Davkaleon strained when Lala referred to the insurance company by name. He'd faced them on several occasions. Was Lala talking about the same company?

"Why did the Flower decide to buy not from me?" Lala returned to the disturbing topic.

"She did not buy. He gifted it to her," replied Tiger, and

nodded towards Davkaleon.

"Davkaleon, what broom did you buy? What's it working on? Clean Force or Dirty Force?" asked Lala.

Davkaleon was stunned. "A broom? What broom? A witch's broom? It is unlikely the girl meant a broom for cleaning the house. And what did Lala mean by asking about Dirty Force? Is it Dark Force or, as they say in Daeya 'Evil Spirits'?"

Davkaleon felt that after DRAGON's drink everything in his head was ringing and noisy, but not to such an extent! When did he manage to buy a witch's broom? Why on earth had he done that? Although it *was* interesting to follow the witch on the witch's Shabash. Especially if this Flower was beautiful.

Davkaleon looked around, Aleurh had already woken up and listened to the revelations about the broom with the same amazement as Davkaleon did. As for Chapius, he slept without waking up. Neither the witch brooms nor the Unclean Forces bothered him.

"Well, you have such an expression of your face!" laughed Aconit, addressing Davkaleon. "Are you afraid of the witch's broom?"

Davkaleon was shocked. Afraid? Him?! In Daeya, the word "afraid" was regarded as a deadly insult. But the girls didn't seem to be trying to offend him. They smiled and made their eyes, so instead of demonstrating resentment, Davkaleon asked: "What is the difference between the brooms working on the Clean Force and the Dirty Force? Which one is better?"

Tiger laughed. "No, just look at that sincere expression

on his face! I have never seen more honest eyes in my life. A little bit more, and I'd believe that he doesn't know the difference between the engines working on Clean Force and Dirty Force."

"Maybe he doesn't remember? Do you remember everything from the school curriculum?" Aconit came to Davkaleon's aid.

"Not everything, of course. But I do remember the fundamental difference between engines that run on Clean Force and those that run on Dirty Force. The ones that run on Clean Force have a bunch of customizable filters. You adjust them as you want, and the engine will get the correct amount of the right quarks and antiquarks, particles and antiparticles, tachyons and anti-tachyons, and all sorts of other stuff, I don't remember what. In those engines that run on the Dirty Force, the engine grabs everything it can, and then figures out what to do with it on its own. If you know in advance the routes you're going to fly, engines on Clean Force are better. Adjust beforehand, and you'll have the fastest broom in the whole world. But if you're going to fly where no broom has ever gone before, you can't do it without a Dirty Force engine," Tiger said.

Davkaleon felt his headache even more from this gibberish. Meanwhile, Lala persistently tried to find out more about the broomstick he'd bought from the competitors.

"Davkaleon, what does the broomstick run on? Don't you know? Or don't you want to tell us? Is it mercury or sulfur?"

"He couldn't have been so *stupid* as to take mercury junk," argued Tiger. "Did you see the ring he gifted Flower? Why would he buy her a broom from the millennium before last? She'd have to refuel at every mercury pump!"

"Not necessarily. You can order a mercury refueler from Witch-net and send the bills to him," Aconit nodded toward Davkaleon.

"Or sign a contract with Witch-net, and they will automatically provide you with refueling on the fly, and you don't even have to stop," Aconit added.

"They will provide, but they will know all your ways and paths. Do you want that?" Tiger grimaced.

"Davkaleon, did you buy from a dealer at a discount or, like the last sucker, at retail?" Lala was interested.

"Wait! Lala interrupted. "Where did you buy it? Is it possible to buy a decent broom in your Daeya? Or did you not get it in Daeya? Hey, you wanna be a dealer? You know, you'd be the exclusive broom supplier for all of Daeya. I'll set you up with a direct contract, along with a witch's loan. And I don't need anything from you, just 1% of each broom. What? One percent is too much? Let us make it half a percent"

Davkaleon was horrified to imagine himself sitting in a store in Daeya, selling brooms to witches. He didn't seem enthusiastic about it. Perhaps his attitude towards selling brooms was too well read on his face, because Lala immediately began to explain the financial side of the matter.

"Do you know how much dealers make on one broom?

20 percent minimum! And if you buy a large batch, 30 percent or even 40 percent!"

Davkaleon grimaced. He made good money, at least by Daeyan standards, but debts always outpaced his earnings, so he was used to dealing with both loans and creditors. Not that the financial side would have anything to do with his reluctance to mess with witches' brooms, but for 20 percent commission? Ha! And the loan, how much would that cost?! And rent? And taxes? And donating the mandatory 10 percent to the temples? He would end up owing money.

Lala seemed to read his mind.

"You don't think 20 percent is enough?! No way! Do you know how much a broom costs? If you have half a percent left after all expenses, you'll be a millionaire in no time. And if you converted it, you'd be laughing at a billion in profit. We're talking about Twierks' *realises*!"

"What's so special about these Twierks' realises?" asked Davkaleon.

"What?" It seems Lala was surprised. "They can be converted into any currency anywhere at any time!"

"He knows it all, he's just pretending," Tiger laughed.

"Lala, are you sure they haven't met yet? How, then, could he have given her a broom?" Aconit hesitated.

"Just like he gave her the ring before," Lala shrugged.

"Let's see if they've met or not," said Aconit as she moved closer to Davkaleon.

"Aconit, you're up for adventure again. Do I have to defend you again?" Tiger asked, seeming ready to jump.

"Tiger, first of all, I'm a witch myself, so I can defend

myself, and secondly, his testosterone is off the charts, and you don't attack girls with that level of hormones. Right, Davkaleon?" Aconit asked, winking.

"It depends on what you mean by attack," Lala said philosophically.

Davkaleon didn't know what the word "testosterone" meant, but he liked the girls, and he obviously wasn't going to attack them. Aconit sang and twirled in a dance.

"Maybe she hasn't met him yet, and he's already met her and gotten to know her," Tiger suggested.

"No, he hasn't," Aconit said confidently, stopping dancing. "See, he's not reacting, and that's Flower's favorite song."

"Then we should check not with a song and dance, but with a sacred phrase," replied Tiger.

"Which one is that?" Aconit asked.

"Heatherochek, coffeeochek," Tiger chanted, looking at Davkaleon.

Davkaleon had never heard the words "Heatherochek" or "coffeeochek," so he didn't react in any way to the so-called sacred phrase.

"Maybe he doesn't like coffee," Lala suggested.

Davkaleon didn't know the word "coffee" either.

"Well, yes, that's because he didn't like coffee, he asked Flower to bring it to him ten times a day," Tiger mocked.

"It had nothing to do with coffee. Flower often brought him coffee in a bikini, that's what he liked," Aconit stated.

"Bikini. What's a bikini? And why do I need that coffee?

What was I doing with it?" Davkaleon whispered. "This is all very confusing." He liked girls, but Davkaleon was used to choosing who he wanted to get to know and who he wanted to court. Here, the girls had taken initiative, and that annoyed him a little. Not a lot...but still! It would have been much better if the girls were whispering quietly among themselves and making eyes at him, as was customary in Daeya. Then he would have chosen. All of them! He liked them all. And his heart was big and kind, enough for all of them.

"Davkaleon, come and sit on the featherbed. It grows in that gazebo over there," Lala said dreamily, coming very close to Davkaleon.

"Ha! You won't seduce him with a featherbed!" Tiger grinned. "He can't sleep on a featherbed! It's too soft for him, and he's not used to it. Flower grew a special mattress for him, something between the bed in his room at the military school and the wooden bench in the cell in the guardhouse. Flower said that he spent more time in the guardhouse than the rest of the school put together. By the way, Davkaleon, what's a guardhouse? I asked Flower, but she couldn't really explain; she said it's where you kill monsters for dinner if you're too lazy to go to the 'Mug and Sword'. And what's a *Mug and Sword*?"

Davkaleon hesitated - had he imagined the girls? They seemed to be aware of his habits. He took another look at Aleurh. The loyal dragon looked as puzzled as he was. He too was wondering if he was dreaming about girls.

"Yes, you are right! Good thing you reminded me," Lala said, taking Davkaleon's hand. "Come, I'll show you your gazebo. Flower told me that you only like cakes for dessert. She's growing pickles and salted tomatoes for you right next to your mattress. And there's brine running from the fountain. It's a great cure. Do you have a headache? Come to the fountain! You'll be cured in no time!"

Davkaleon hesitated. He wanted to go, but the whole situation was just too implausible. On the other hand, from the moment he, Chapius and Aleurh had entered the Mage Chamber and from there into the DRAGON Corridor, *everything* had been implausible. Davkaleon took a step towards the gazebo. Faithful Aleurh growled warningly. Tiger walked up to Aleurh and said: "Green, don't growl. Better come with us; you try it, it'll fix you up too." Aleurh growled more quietly, he even let Tiger pet him. After another minute, he was purring affectionately as Tiger stroked his scruff.

"Drink from this fountain," Lala suggested to Davkaleon. "And then you," the girl turned, and pointed at Aleurh.

Davkaleon liked the brine. The noise in his head lessened. Aleurh also approved of the drink, too.

"Try the pickle. Salty. Flower grows them right here. Maybe you're hungry?" Lala asked thoughtfully.

Davkaleon lifted his head up. It wasn't that he was hungry, but something colorful, of a decent size, was singing a song very close by. If you reached out and built a fire, it would make a nice addition to Flower's pickles.

"Don't touch the songbird. Flower will die. She might even be late for the wedding," said Lala, pointing to a white table in the shape of a barrel. "Flower has grown a special mushroom for you."

"Mushroom? Are you kidding! He wants meat. He'll only be interested in mushrooms as an appetizer," Tiger grinned.

"It depends on what kind of mushroom," Lala said, lifting the lid of the barrel table.

The wonderful smell of fried meat with Davkaleon's favorite seasonings spread around.

"The fried mushroom grows inside, and it's always warm. And if you eat the whole thing, a new one grows instantly. And the plates and utensils grow here too," Lala explained, holding out a portion of mushrooms to the astonished Davkaleon.

"Green, help yourself, there's enough for everyone," Tiger offered, turning to Aleurh.

The mushrooms tasted exactly like Davkaleon's favorite dish.

"Whose wedding will Flower be late for?" Davkaleon asked. Not that he was very interested, but he wanted to keep the conversation going.

"To *yours*, of course," Lala answered, holding out more mushrooms.

Davkaleon froze, holding his fork with a bite of mushroom.

"Davkaleon, don't eat too many mushrooms. You'll ruin your appetite, and you're in for such a treat, it'll make your mouth water," Aconit promised. "What a coven we're going to have. The whole of Twierks is getting ready. It's not every day a Twierks witch marries in full Twierks rites."

"Yeah, we'll be having a coven like this for at least two weeks," Tiger said dreamily.

"A Twierks witch?! I'm marrying a Twierks witch?!" Davkaleon looked back at Aleurh helplessly. The faithful dragon looked completely dumbfounded.

"Not just any witch, but a *certified* Twierks witch," Lala said proudly.

"What do you mean, a certified witch? And why do I need her?" Davkaleon couldn't get over it.

"Why? Imagine, your wife is a certified scholarly witch. No one else has one, but you do. You'll be proud to hang the certificate on your bedroom wall," Aconit added.

Davkaleon remembered the last lesson of the bald little Mr. Pusik. "Remember, there's nothing worse than a scholarly witch!" Pusik, the etiquette teacher, had insisted.

"Don't pretend it was an accident. Do you think anyone in Twierks believes that you didn't plan to marry a Twierks witch from the start? Ha! You even agreed to a full Twierks wedding rite. You know, that's not something a lot of people agree to," Tiger said.

"What kind of rite is this?" Davkaleon was worried.

"No one knows for sure. There are several rooms in the Twierks' Depository filled with explanatory documents, but only those who have agreed to the rite beforehand are allowed in. You were taken there yesterday, spent two minutes there, signed the Twierks contract without reading, and said that you were ready to marry Flower any time with any rite and ritual," Lala explained.

"You can do a better job of explaining what this rite is," Aleurh said, expressing obvious concern for Davkaleon's fate.

"I have no idea how to explain it," Lala sighed. "But I can tell you this...some people survive!" Lala smiled.

"Don't scare him before his time; he still has to get away from the goblins, get out of the Earth, and jump into the quantizer," Tiger said.

Davkaleon didn't know what a quantizer was, so he didn't associate that word with any danger. He had faced goblins many times and always defeated them. But it was the word "Earth" that left Davkaleon utterly confused. He had been told in Daeya that Earth was the shadow world tied to Daeya, and it was impossible to get to Earth if you were alive. And if by some miracle you ended up on Earth when you were alive, there was no going back to Daeya.

Aconit interpreted Davkaleon's confusion in her own way. "Don't try to play the 'I'm not me, and the idea is not mine' card, and wipe that 'I don't remember anything, I don't know anything' expression off your face. You won't convince anyone at Twierks with that. We're pretty sure you somehow found a way to the Depository and read the documents beforehand, unless you signed them without looking," Aconit added mockingly. "If that weren't true, you wouldn't have spent five hours traveling to Earth. All you had to do was dive into a tachyon tunnel, and you'd be on Earth in a heartbeat. But no, you didn't do it, you see. Ha! We believed you! You just wanted to wait for Flower to become a Twierks witch." And with a graceful wave of her hands, Aconit sang:

You did not want just witch of Llilll,
You desired witch of Twierks.
Why are you surprised now?
Why are you amazed by witchcraft tricks?

"Why do I need a Twierks' witch?! What's the difference between a Llill's witch and a Twierks' witch?" Davkaleon asked, astonished.

Lala, Tiger, and Aconit burst out laughing. Suddenly, three broomsticks appeared. The girls jumped on them and circled around Davkaleon. Then, in the blink of an eye, they rose to their full height and danced on their brooms. Mesmerized, Davkaleon watched the witches perform their dance.

"Lala! Where did you transport them to?" a voice came from the right.

The newcomer, a slightly older yet equally attractive girl, appeared.

"To Twierks, to Flower's corner," Lala replied nonchalantly.

"And where did I instruct you to go?" questioned the newcomer.

"Loveliness, you didn't give me any instructions! You handed me a note with two orders! I apologize; I haven't completed them yet. But I'll fulfill them as soon as I deliver these ... By the way, where should I deliver them?" Lala asked.

"Lala, the note I gave you wasn't about the orders, it was about moving coordinates," Loveliness clarified. "Return them to Pillentally cave in Daeya."

A black vortex swooped in, swiftly swirling, and

spinning Davkaleon around, before dropping him near the exit of Pillentally Cave. Beside him lay his faithful dragon, Chapius, peacefully asleep. Had Davkaleon truly visited Twierks and encountered the girls, or had it all been a figment of his imagination?

Davkaleon turned to Aleurh. "Did you see them?" he asked.

"I've had too much DRAGON's drink, so I don't know," Aleurh replied uncertainly.

"But I saw Lala, and Tiger, and Aconit. And then I saw Loveliness. And I heard about Flower with the broom! And the wedding!"

"You need a girl, because you see tigers with witches' brooms," Aleurh teased. Then he added, "As for me, I want a dragoness. A young one." "Have you heard anything about *heatherocheck* or *coffeeocheck*?" Davkaleon asked Chapius, shaking his friend awake.

"About what?" Chapius clearly didn't understand.

"You see, while you were sleeping, I talked to the witches. They told me that I was about to be married, but that I had not yet met the bride."

"You are strange, Davkaleon," said Chapius. "You have agreed to marry, though you have not yet met the bride. What if you don't like her?"

"What makes you think that I will marry without looking?" Davkaleon was surprised.

"You said so."

"No, no, you misunderstood. That's what the witches told me, but I haven't agreed yet. Besides, they told me a so-called sacred phrase, but I have no idea what a sacred phrase is or what it means."

"And what is this phrase?" Chapius asked.

"Heatherochek, coffeeochek," Davkaleon repeated what he had heard from Tiger.

"It's simple," replied Chapius. "Heatherochek is the diminutive of Heather, and coffeeochek is coffee. Only, I don't know what coffee is. Remember when I told you about my mom calling me Chapa-shka? It's the same thing."

"Wow, it's the same thing. What do Chapa-shka and Heatherochek have in common?"

"People tack endings onto names to show affection," Chapius explained. "One word has one ending, and another has a different ending. Heather will be Heather-ochek because Heather-shka doesn't sound good. I, on the contrary, Chapa-shka sounds good, but Chapa-ochek...well, no way. And with your name, you could be Davkaleon-chik and Davkaleon-ushka."

"No, I'm Davkaleon. I don't need to add any endings to my name! Are you sure Heatherochek is Heather?"

"I don't know if she is the Heather you're thinking of, but it's a diminutive of Heather."

"Her! Of course, her," Davkaleon smiled. "Why would I agree to anyone else?"

*****

Davkaleon rushed in to see his brother Elfid at the first opportunity.

"Are you sure it was about you and Heather?" Elfid asked when Davkaleon had recounted what had happened.

"Of course, it was!" Davkaleon answered confidently. "The witches recognized me and called me by name."

"That's strange," replied Elfid. "Only Twierks mages and Twierks witches can marry according to the full Twierks rite. Even Llill priestesses can't do it. For this to happen, Heather must undergo all the steps in her training and be initiated by the Twierks Council. As for you, you must become a Twierks mage."

"All right, let's say it happens," Davkaleon replied. "What is the meaning of this rite?"

"Only those who have been through the rite can answer that question. The point is that it is forbidden to divulge any information about it," Elfid answered. "The only thing I can tell you is that if, by some miracle, you hope to become a Twierks mage, you'd better skip the brides' ball in Daeya. The full Twierks rite requires monogamy."

"What the hell is that?" Davkaleon asked.

"A woman has only one husband," Elfid began to explain.

"Naturally!!! How else could it be?"

"A man has only one wife."

"One?! But she'll be bored!" Davkaleon was genuinely surprised. "Look at how well our family is doing. Father is at work, and his wives visit each other, show each other outfits, tell each other the news, play cards. It's fun!"

Elfid shook his head.

*****

"Are you sure your Davkaleon is that into Heather? I think he's doing just fine without her," Adamant grinned.

"Let's get him to meet her and see how much he's into her," Ecktoral suggested.

"You said he's almost eighteen, how old is she?"

"She's about to be 13."

"That's too young. She could use a little more growing up."

"Ha! Big problem. Let's move her forward a couple years," Ecktoral shrugged.

The school of priestesses of the goddess ISIDA appeared on the wall screen: The Exam of the ISIDE Students.

* * * * *

"There are those who have successfully answered the test questions," said priestess Mistletoe. "You have one last test remaining: a practical exam. After that, you will move on to the next level," she continued.

The girls sat in Mistletoe's office around a long table, at arm's length.

"Each of you will pass the exam with the help of an Exasizer," the priestess explained, nodding towards the Exasizer standing on the table.

"Why, call an ordinary computer an Exasizer?" Tiger whispered.

Priestess Mistletoe either did not hear or pretended not to hear Tiger's comment. "The task for you is to correctly identify the danger threatening you and take the necessary actions to eliminate it. Since you're familiar with various amulets and artifacts, you know how to protect yourself. Your duplicate in the Exasizer will precisely replicate your actions. You won't even have to say anything; just think about it."

"Wow, this Exasizer is better than any gaming computer," Tiger remarked.

The priestess Mistletoe approached the nearest student. "Maya, you've had problems with the magic kitchen before. You attempted to add fly agaric poison to the drink of our esteemed guests."

"Esteemed guests?!" Maya exclaimed. "Those scoundrels ruined my entire dress at the ball!"

"Maya, it wasn't them. It was a cat."

"Whose cat was it?" Maya remained unconvinced.

"Let's leave the cat aside for now. Look at the Exasizer. Do you recognize yourself? You're in the kitchen. Tiger and Heather are preparing a surprise dish and are unaware that one of the students is about to throw Lemon Triktis into the hall, but you can see it. You need to act swiftly to stop him, but using fly agaric poison isn't necessary. This is your task, and you have a few minutes to think while I assign tasks to the other students."

"There's nothing to think about. A frying pan to the head, and problem solved," Maya responded.

"Maya, you've been taking Miss Loveliness's lessons for so long," priestess Mistletoe said reproachfully, "you ought to devise a more elegant solution."

"I can make it elegant," Maya promised. "For instance, I could say, *I was just about to offer our esteemed guest special gloves to prevent any burns while handling his Lemon Triktis, but at that moment a large cast-iron frying pan slipped from my grasp. Regrettably, it landed right on his head.*"

"Maya, do you realize you'll be graded on this exam?" the priestess asked.

"Okay, okay. I'll make it even more elegant," Maya agreed.

"Now, Iya, it's your turn," priestess Mistletoe said as she approached the next girl.

"My name is Aconit," Iya replied.

"Wonderful, Aconit. Let's see how you handle your challenge. Imagine you're returning home for the holidays. However, we'll skip the initial reunion with your parents and jump straight to the point where a Difeserant arrives at your doorstep. He will demand that your parents offer you up for sacrifice. Remember, the Difeserant is afraid of fire, and you have amulets that can emit flames. Consider your options and demonstrate your actions to us."

Mistletoe then approached Heather. "Your exam will be without an Exasizer. You have a rendezvous on the night of Lughnasadh at the fountain behind the temple. However, it's all within your imagination, and your mystery prince is unaware of it. But the Difeserant *is* aware. The Difeserant might not be alone. You need to prepare for this encounter. How many flame-spewing bracelets do you possess?"

"Two, one on each arm," Heather replied.

"That's not sufficient. Take another pair," Mistletoe advised, handing over the bracelets.

"I have nowhere left to wear them," Heather complained, displaying her hands adorned with magic bracelets and rings.

Mistletoe ignored her complaints. "I'll send you to the

fountain. I've already set the time and location on the Clock of the Mages. See the clock by the wall? Prepare yourself to confront multiple Difeserants simultaneously. I want you to handle it yourself, but if there are too many Difeserants, don't worry. I'll be there. Another Clock of Mages will be positioned near the fountain. They will be programmed to return you to the temple. I'll render them invisible. If everything proceeds smoothly, you won't need to use them. However, if anything goes awry, the Clock will assist you."

Mistletoe approached Tiger.

"Let's imagine that you and Heather are in the midst of preparing your Surprised Drink, and the very student magician who swapped out your medallion enters your kitchen. This time, he attempts to replace one of your amulet bracelets. Think over your actions and demonstrate them."

"I don't need amulets for this. My kung-fu will suffice," Tiger declared.

After distributing tasks to several more students, priestess Mistletoe returned to Maya. "Are you ready?" The priestess asked. "Let's get started."

And Maya began. Honey and molasses dripped over the ears of the imaginary guest. "Greetings, O cleverest of the clever, the best of the best, the worthiest among students of mages. It is a pleasure to see you here," Maya greeted the guest. "I have a delightful surprise dish featuring mushrooms. Would you like to try it?" Maya pressed one of her many rings. A wisp of smoke drifted from the ring towards the future mage.

"Maya, I warned you about using mushrooms or poison!" The priestess Mistletoe exclaimed.

"It's not poison at all! It's simply a hallucinogenic spray, meant to make him believe what I'm saying immediately. And I mentioned the mushroom just to set up the surprise," Maya retorted.

"Very well, continue," the priestess Mistletoe graciously permitted.

"Oh no, why did your finger fall off?" Maya exclaimed, her eyes widening in fear as she glanced at the guest.

The imaginary guest looked down in surprise, noticing that indeed, one finger was missing from his hand!

"And now another finger from the other hand!" Maya gasped, feigning a dramatic clutch at her heart.

The guest inspected his other hand, bewildered by the sudden loss.

"Let me hold your Triktis," Maya offered, reaching for the bottle in the visitor's hand. She aimed a bottle of Lemon Triktis at the guest, but the priestess Mistletoe shook her head disapprovingly. Setting the bottle aside, Maya refocused on her guest.

"You're falling apart everywhere! Look, all your fingers are scattered on the floor!" she exclaimed, pointing to the ground.

The girls watched the show with keen interest. Heather rose from her seat to get a better view. As her fire-shooting bracelets connected, flames surged towards the ceiling. The priestess Mistletoe hurried to Heather and swiftly removed her newly adorned bracelets.

"Perhaps two of yours are sufficient," the priestess remarked.

While the priestess was preoccupied with Heather, Maya seized the opportunity. She winked at the other girls and whispered something to the student of mages. The unfortunate guest watched in horror as his fingers leapt off the floor into the frying pan.

"Let's throw in some onions," Maya suggested cheerfully.

Setting aside the bracelets, Mistletoe turned to Maya with concern. "What have you done to him? Why does he look so pale?" the priestess inquired.

"I intended to surprise him with a dish, but he must be allergic to onions," Maya explained.

"Then remove the onions," Mistletoe advised.

"Of course," Maya agreed, promptly removing the offending ingredient from the pan. However, the guest's condition didn't improve.

"It seems he's not allergic to onions, but perhaps to the main course," Maya lamented.

"Okay," Mistletoe waved her hand, "he'll have to manage his allergies on his own. Do you have a bottle of Lemon Triktis?"

"Of course!" Maya responded proudly.

"In that case, you've passed!"

Maya beamed, and the priestess turned her attention to the rest of the students.

"Attention, everyone," the priestess announced. "In Maya's demonstration, the magician's apprentice didn't attempt to resist. However, real-life scenarios won't be so easy. Consider this your initial exposure to the Exasizer, so for now, I'm solely observing your actions. As you progress, you'll encounter more intricate modes with the Exasizer."

The priestess Mistletoe approached Iya-Aconit. "Let's get started," she said.

The girl found herself in her parents' house. The first few minutes were pleasant; she was surrounded by her loved ones. Then the door swung open, and a sinister figure in a black cape with a hood appeared in the doorway.

"I'm here for the girl," the Difeserant growled rudely as he approached Iya-Aconit, "your family has neglected their sacred duties for too long."

Iya screamed and rushed towards the back door. Her father attempted to detain the Difeserant, but in response, the Difeserant lifted him to the ceiling and squeezed his throat.

"Let him go!" Iya's mother screamed as she rushed towards the monster.

Iya turned around. Bloodshot, malevolent eyes glared at her. "Come here," the monster said with a grin, "or I'll strangle him."

Iya took a step forward. Extending her hands adorned with bracelets, she directed a barrage of fire at the monster. The monster flung Iya's father away and reached out its elongated paws, attempting to intercept Iya's hands. The fire intensified, and the monster was propelled backward. Struggling to get up, it limped away. The flames from Iya's hands pursued it.

Iya froze, scarcely able to believe what had just occurred. Then, throwing her hands up, she screamed, "I did it! I actually did it! Oh, ISIDA, thank you! I've done it now!" Iya began to dance.

"Now I'm Aconit! Now I am a true witch's flower Aconit! I'm not afraid of anything! I'm not afraid of anyone!"

"Iya, what's happening to you? What do you mean by Aconit? Are you talking about flowers?" The girl's mother was concerned.

Next to Iya's house, several aconit flowers grew. In Attl, it was believed that the aconite flower always thrived near a witch's dwelling. Despite her mother's attempts to uproot the flowers multiple times, they stubbornly regrew each time. Iya always felt a sense of pity for the beautiful blue flowers, and she secretly replanted the uprooted plants back into their place.

"Yes, I am an aconit flower," Iya laughed and sang.

The witch's flower, aconit, bloomed and burned there.

Iya sang and danced. Iya-Aconit danced on the screen, mirroring her movements in the room. Her wild dance captivated everyone. With a wave of her hand, Aconit touched the arrows on the Mage's Clock. The arrows swayed forward as Aconit continued to dance, then swung back, forward again and back once more.

"Oh, what is it?" Heather screamed.

Her head was spinning. Heather looked at her reflection on the Exasizer screen. But was it really her? A little girl stood near the sandbox at her father's estate and looked at her oversized dress in surprise. It was obviously too big for her. It seemed as though the dress was about to slip off. In the next instant, the girl's age changed. Heather clutched at her dress, feeling it tightening around her chest, hips, and waist.

"Stop! Freeze!" echoed the desperate cry of priestess Mistletoe to Iya-Aconit, but Aconit did not hear her.

With a few more steps, Aconit reached out and touched the Eye of the Gods. The crystal ball then began to slowly float across the room. Stunned, Heather stared at herself in the ball. She saw herself as a little girl, playing with her brother in her father's estate near the sandbox. Now, she found herself fighting off a Difeserant at the magicians' apprentice tournament, only to be transported back to the familiar scene near the sandbox. The crystal ball showed her Davkaleon—known to her as Alfreydon— who was in the thick of the battle with someone preparing to throw a spear at him from behind.

With mounting desperation, Heather screamed at the top of her voice, Look around!"

Heather screamed so loudly that Alfreydon glanced back. He swiftly dodged the spear aimed at him. Catching each other's gaze for a fleeting moment, Alfreydon then plunged into battle. Heather, in awe of his strength and bravery, watched with bated breath as he confronted multiple adversaries single-handedly. His foes were accompanied by monstrous creatures resembling fire-breathing dragons. Although Heather had never encountered dragons herself, she had seen depictions of them.

Fixating on the Exasizer, Heather noticed the familiar landscape of her father's estate visible within. Without hesitation, she darted towards it, scooped up a handful of sand, and hurled it into the eyes of one of the fire-breathing dragons. The creature staggered and shook its head. Heather repeated the action, targeting another dragon with sand, causing it to pause momentarily. Suddenly, the image within the crystal ball began to fade, and the ball soared away.

"Heather, what are you doing?" Tiger exclaimed, brushing grains of sand off her dress, but she received no response.

Iya- Aconit danced with her eyes closed, oblivious to her surroundings.

"Aconit, calm down!" Priestess Mistletoe exclaimed, grasping the girl's hand. Before she could fully comprehend the situation, Aconit inadvertently brushed against a large, gilded key on the Mages' Clock, causing Heather to vanish from the room.

"Where's Heather?" Aconit asked in bewilderment, scanning the area.

"I think the *real* question is, where did you send her?" Tiger demanded.

"Let's see," priestess Mistletoe responded, assured that Heather was attending to her task at the fountain. The priestess approached the Exasizer. The device displayed Difeserant, appearing bewildered as he glanced around.

"Where did she go?" The priestess exclaimed, surprised. "I hope she remembered the position of the arrows on the night of the Lughnasadh.

"What if there's no Mages' Clock where she ends up?" Tiger interjected.

"In that case, she won't be able to return on her own," Mistletoe replied.

"And then what? Will she be lost?" Tiger pressed.

"An envoy will need to be dispatched for her."

"Can I be the envoy?" Tiger inquired.

"If you retrieve the silver arrow, yes, but don't disturb me at the moment. Finding her takes precedence," Mistletoe replied, taking hold of the crystal ball.

"What's happening?" The priestess whispered in astonishment as she examined the Eye of the Goddess.

"What's going on?" the girls approached, curious.

"Everyone is dismissed. We'll resume the examination later. Leave now," the priestess commanded.

Left alone, Mistletoe focused on the crystal ball once more. Heather briefly appeared, only to vanish again. The priestess waved her hand over the ball, peering intently. Heather flickered into view once more before disappearing completely.

"Why was the recording erased?" Mistletoe muttered in disbelief.

"Mage Eximi," the priestess addressed the mage's reflection within the crystal ball, "Your protégé has vanished, and the Eye of the Goddess fails to reveal her."

"Is she missing?" Eximi exclaimed in surprise. "Hold on, let me locate her."

After a few moments, Eximi spoke again. "I've found her. Don't fret, she's not lost."

"Should we send someone to retrieve her?" the priestess

inquired.

"No need. I'll handle it personally. You will meet her on the night of the Lughnasad as planned." Eximi assured.

*****

"And now it's time to grab some popcorn and watch their encounter. I'm a sucker for romance," Ecktoral said dreamily.

"Just don't drag out their meeting into a month-long soap opera," Adamant remarked with a yawn.

*****

Heather found herself beside the fountain next to the temple, where malevolent eyes of the Difeserant stared at her. "Where is your Abal-Dural?" The Difeserant growled.

A dragon with a warrior materialized to her right. Heather had been prepared to encounter the Difeserant, but not a dragon. She quickly jumped aside.

"Are you waiting for Abal-Dural? I'm here!" the warrior shouted, swinging his sword at the Difeserant.

Heather hadn't expected to meet the mythical Abal-Dural at all. What surprised her even more was that the warrior who appeared bore a striking resemblance to Alfreydon. Had the goddess ISIDA sent her a protector without her even asking? Heather pointed her bracelet at the Difeserant but immediately lowered her hand. "I might harm Alfreydon," she thought, filled with fear.

Alfreydon and his dragon executed a splendid job on their own. However, one of them accidentally brushed against the Clock of the Mages. The hands on the Clock swirled, and another dragon warrior materialized on the left.

"Greetings from Abal-Dural!" he exclaimed with laughter.

Whether it was the same warrior or different one, Heather couldn't discern. The hands on the Clock were spinning widely, so it might have been the same warrior on the same dragon, just a moment earlier or later.

Another Abal-Dural emerged near the Clock. And then another one. However, Heather's head was spinning from the sight, so she couldn't be certain.

"I think I failed the exam," she thought. "I need to reset the Mage's Clock so that I can go back a few minutes and have time to use the flame–spewing bracelets, as required by the task. However, this plan did not work out for Heather; a Difeserant appeared next to the Clock. Heather attempted to reset the Clock mentally. Mistletoe had shown the students how to do it, but the arrows did not obey.

"A spell! I have to cast a spell," she thought. "And I must calculate the formula. I need to determine the difference between the current time and the time I need. But what is the current time?"

The arrows of the Clock continued to fluctuate, making

it difficult to determine the current time. A Difeserant reached out a paw to Heather. The arrows of the Clock swung again, and Heather suddenly found herself inside the temple. Looking around, she realized it was an unfamiliar temple.

"Where is the Clock of the Mages? How am I going to get back?" the thought raced through her mind.

A tall guy stood near a column, bearing a striking resemblance to the dragon warrior at the fountain.

"Heather?!" the guy exclaimed with delight.

"Alfreydon?" Heather smiled happily and added. "Oh, ISIDA the great, thank you, you always come to my aid."

*****

"Is this your Davkaleon?" Adamant inquired.

"That's him. And we've returned to Daeya," Ecktoral replied. "Now let's observe his devotion to Heather and evaluate my expertise in the art of matchmaking."

"What is Davkaleon-Alfreydon doing in the temple of ISIDA?" Adamant asked impatiently.

"Don't jump to conclusions. I'll explain everything shortly."

Chapter 10. Meeting with Heather

A skirmish erupted with the Adoleeseets on the outskirts of Daeya. Senior classes at the military school were suspended, and students were informed that a combat mission awaited them. Davkaleon and his classmates eagerly anticipated their deployment location. Dragons also congregated, curious as to why the announcement of their flight destination was delayed. While this wasn't their first experience being dispatched to battle zones, the prolonged wait seemed unusual.

"It's been rumored that there are only a few Adoleeseets left. Perhaps they've already dealt with them without our intervention, which could explain the delay in our orders," speculated one of the students.

"Perhaps. In that case, they could have let us know we're free to head to the *Mug and Sword*. I'm already famished," another remarked.

The *Mug and Sword* was the favored tavern among all the students of the military school, and its mention sparked excitement. Lunchtime had long passed, and everyone's stomachs rumbled with hunger.

Finally, Captain Harding emerged and announced their deployment to Llill.

"To Llill? Have the Adoleeseets reached Llill?" students asked. Although Llill wasn't situated in the heart of Daeya, it was far from the outskirts.

"No, the Adoleeseets haven't reached Llill. However, there are witnesses claiming that the witches of Llill colluded with the Adoleeseets, providing them with information about the movements of Daeya's troops,"

Captain Harding explained.

"How did the witches come to know about our troop movements?"

"What do you mean *how*? They're witches! They know everything," one of the students retorted.

Davkaleon shrugged. "Did etiquette teacher Pusik tell you that? Do you see scholarly witches lurking around every corner?"

"It's not as straightforward with Llill, Davkaleon," Captain Harding interjected. "There was a small Daeya squad stationed in Llill. In recent days, nearly all of them have perished. Those who survived have recounted unbelievable tales."

"What sort of tales?"

"I will personally speak with those who are still alive. Then, we'll reconvene to discuss further," Harding replied, signaling to prepare for departure.

*****

A few survivors from Llill recounted what appeared to be instances of black magic. Uncertainty shrouded the identity of their assailants. The attack occurred under the cover of night, catching the guards off guard as the enemies materialized out of thin air. Initially resembling Svargs, they were nearly all killed, but the unsettling twist came when the slain Svargs inexplicably returned to life.

"What do witches have to do with this?" some asked.

"Only black magicians and witches have the power to resurrect the dead," argued some.

"Black magicians perhaps, but not witches," countered others.

The flames of suspicion were stoked further by a witness who claimed to have seen a Llill witch resurrecting a Svarg. Hours later, news arrived that Daeya's priests had declared a holy war against witches.

While some responded with indifference, many expressed misgivings. "Do we have to fight women now?" they asked, their displeasure palpable.

Among the Daeyans, Llill had always been associated with endless holidays, delectable cuisine, enchanting magic, and the captivating sorceresses of Llill, whom the priests labeled as witches. Few were eager to engage in conflict with them. However, tensions escalated rapidly. Several women sought sanctuary in the temple. An eyewitness, who arrived in a flurry, claimed to have witnessed the witches resurrecting the slain Svargs. Yet, the eyewitness vanished shortly afterward. Despite this, Captain Harding ordered the temple to be entered and all those seeking refuge to be gathered in one place.

"What next?" Davkaleon asked, his displeasure evident.

"Shut up," Harding snapped rudely, displaying his own discomfort with the situation.

Reluctantly, Davkaleon entered the temple with the others. The women had already gathered in one place, with no Svargs in sight.

"We need to thoroughly inspect the entire temple," Harding ordered.

Davkaleon moved behind the columns, feeling far from enthusiastic about the task. This wasn't how he had envisioned the beginning of his military career. Suddenly, a girlish silhouette appeared near the column, and in the next moment, Davkaleon recognized the golden-haired girl. Heather!

"Alfreydon?" Heather smiled warmly, then added with a hint of gratitude, "Oh, ISIDA the great, thank you. You always come to my aid."

It was the first time Davkaleon had seen the girl without a mask, yet he was certain it was her. A whirlwind of emotions churned in his chest. Until now, their encounters had been fleeting, always under urgent circumstances, leaving them no time for conversation. The only change this time was Heather's unmasked face. The circumstances remained dire.

"A Difeserant is pursuing me. Do you know where the

Mages' Clock is?" Heather asked urgently. "I must rearrange them before he catches up."

"Don't fear the Difeserant. I'll dispatch him swiftly," Davkaleon reassured her. Difeserants didn't trouble him much; he had battled them frequently over the past few years. Though the concept of the Mages' Clock was unfamiliar, it paled in comparison to his concern for Heather's safety. He couldn't leave her in the temple, but where could he hide her? Taking Heather's hand, Davkaleon guided her through the side door of the temple.

As they approached Aleurh, Heather's eyes widened with apprehension at the sight of the dragon.

"Don't be afraid! This is the kindest dragon in the world!" Davkaleon reassured her earnestly. "He will protect you from all the Difeserants, Svargs, and any other monsters."

"Aleurh, this is *my* Heather," Davkaleon offered, emphasizing the possessive. "I've spoken of her to you."

Aleurh tilted his head, regarding the girl with curiosity. He had heard of Heather before. Seeing her in person, rather than merely hearing about her in Davkaleon's tales, was a novel experience. After all, it was about time someone appeared in his friend's life. And if Davkaleon held Heather in such high regard, who was Aleurh to question it? Yet, the timing of her appearance in Llill, amidst Daeya's call for a holy war against witches, gave pause for thought. It was evident to anyone at first glance that she was a witch. Her beauty alone was evidence enough. No wonder Davkaleon was so taken with her.

"Aleurh, fly her to Assa. Here's the money; rent the best

accommodation in the safest area," Davkaleon instructed firmly.

"Are you out of your mind? Assa is hours away by flight. Let's hide her in the caves near Llill," Aleurh countered.

"What are you suggesting? Leaving her alone in a cave? What if a hungry monster appears? No, she needs to be taken to Assa," Davkaleon insisted.

"This is desertion!" Aleurh cried.

"No, I've considered everything! Once you've settled Heather in, go to Elfid, inform him of the situation, and give him this note," Davkaleon said, hastily scribbling a few words on a piece of papyrus. Aleurh glanced at the note:

"Elfid, you spoke to me about the transformations of the Difeserants, mentioning they resembled the revival of the dead. Can Svargs perform such feats, and how should we address it?"

"This note will absolve you of any suspicion. I'll inform Harding about it once you and Heather depart. If Harding is displeased, I'll take the blame. By the time you receive this note, you'll already believe we've discussed it with Harding," Davkaleon assured.

"And what pleasure would it bring me to stay at school alone, watching you face a trial?" Aleurh objected.

"They won't subject me to a trial. At worst, I'll be confined to the guardhouse," Davkaleon replied dismissively.

Though Aleurh remained stubborn, Davkaleon eventually managed to sway him. "Please, find her the safest place to reside and hire a guard." Davkaleon requested as he made his way toward Captain Harding.

*****

"Since when do you take matters into your own hands and then inform me about them?" Captain Harding fumed as Davkaleon informed him of sending Aleurh with a note to Elfid. "Sixty days in the guardhouse for each of you and consider yourselves lucky I didn't send you both to court."

"Aleurh had no part in this. He believed I was acting under your authority," Davkaleon insisted.

"So, you deceived your dragon as well! Another sixty days!" Harding snapped back.

"I didn't deceive him intentionally. I was so convinced you would approve that I acted as though it was already settled. It never crossed my mind that Aleurh thought otherwise," Davkaleon tried to explain, attempting to maneuver out of the situation.

"Ah, so it never crossed your dragon's mind that you acted without permission! Apparently, he doesn't know you at all. According to him, you're an exceptionally obedient student. He must be unaware that you spend more time in the guardhouse than the entire school combined," Harding raged.

Then, to Davkaleon's surprise, Captain Harding calmed down rather swiftly. 120 days seemed like a paltry punishment, especially considering he only had two months left in school. Surely, they wouldn't confine him to the guardhouse after graduation. Or would they?

Suddenly, a stranger burst out of the temple and

dashed towards Captain Harding. "The Llill witch revived a Svarg, I witnessed it!" he insisted. "Then she vanished from the temple, but I can still smell her. She was with him!" He pointed accusingly at Davkaleon. "Where is she?"

"Do you rely on your sense of smell? Are you some kind of animal?" Davkaleon seethed, his temper flaring. "And how did you even enter the temple? You're not a Daeyan; you're a damned Difeserant!"

"Stop!" Captain Harding's command came too late. Davkaleon had already unsheathed his sword and struck the "smeller." Brown liquid gushed onto the ground, but it hardly resembled blood.

"What is this?" Harding, who had never encountered a Difeserant before, recoiled in astonishment. Several appendages emerged from the Difeserant's body, grappling with Davkaleon. Harding swung his sword, severing one of the creature's arms, but another quickly sprouted in its place. Spectators watched in disbelief as the wounds on the Difeserant's body healed, and the severed appendage wriggled its way back to its master. Another arm grew in place where the severed arm had been thrown too far away.

"Who is Elfid, and why did you send the note to him?" Harding asked Davkaleon a few minutes later.

"He's my brother. He studies at the School of Sciences. If Elfid is nearby, there's no need for a library. He's read all the manuscripts and scrolls available in Daeya and has shared many unexpected insights about the Difeserants. I asked him if the Svargs could come to life like the Difeserants, and how to prevent it."

"Alright, let's see," Captain Harding grumbled. "If Elfid offers something worthwhile, then perhaps you get a dozen days."

Davkaleon knew that only fire could deal with a Difeserant. He had learned this during his first visit to the temple in the rock. But he wanted Elfid to suggest it. A dozen days in the guardhouse was much better than 120, especially if Heather was waiting for him at the Assa.

A few hours later, Aleurh delivered a note from Elfid.

"A Difeserants can pretend to be anyone, including Svarg and Daeyan. It can only be destroyed by fire. Keep in mind, if a partially burned stub of a finger remains somewhere, then a new Difeserants will grow out of it alive and unharmed in a few hours," Elfid wrote.

"Okay, you're going to serve three days, so you remember to report before you do something, not after," Captain Harding told Davkaleon. "And now let's get to work. So, that not a single piece of this abomination remains. Our dragons will do a great job with this."

"I found her a place to live," Aleurh whispered, "and left the Hydragon with her. He must be of some use."

The Hydragon was once a three-headed baby hydra, but those cub days were long gone. Now, he was Davkaleon's fully grown three-year-old pet. Davkaleon had saved him once, and since then, the Hydragon shamelessly exploited Davkaleon's affection. Although he could have hunted on his own for a long time, he preferred playing cards with himself, utilizing his three heads, and leaving the dangerous task of hunting to his master. Unlike other hydras, the Hydragon could breathe fire. It wasn't as potent as a dragon's, but it was still fire, causing the other hydras to not consider him one of their own. As for dragons, they wouldn't accept a three-headed freak into their ranks, especially one capable of only exhaling feeble sparks instead of an endless stream of flames. Most likely, the Hydragon was a crossbreed between a hydra and a dragon, although both species vehemently denied such a possibility.

"Wasn't Heather scared?" Davkaleon asked.

"Only at the beginning. Then the Hydragon invited her to play cards and started teaching her. He also mentioned that you owe him lunch, but that's nothing new. This glutton is always too lazy to hunt for himself," Aleurh explained.

"Yes, one more thing," Aleurh whispered, "I had to inform Elfid about Heather. Otherwise, he wouldn't understand why you were asking him about Svargs and Difeserants when you already know all about them."

"It's okay. Elfid is already aware of her," Davkaleon answered.

Nevertheless, Captain Harding ordered the witches to be transported from the Llill Temple to the capital of Daeya Assa.

"What can I do?" Harding snapped at the questions pouring in. "The priests want to see them. The last witness turned out to be a Difeserant, but among the witnesses, there are a couple of ordinary Daeyans, and they claim that the witches aided the Svargs."

Chapter 11. Heather's Story

Davkaleon managed to exchange a few words with Heather before heading to the guardhouse. However, he slipped away from the guardhouse as soon as everyone fell asleep. Luckily, he was familiar with all the maneuvers and exits.

"Davkaleon, did you bring any food? I'm quite hungry," Hydragon asked in a pleading tone as soon as Davkaleon crossed the threshold.

"Hungry? What are you saying?! Go hunt and bring back food for us."

"What are you talking about, Davkaleon? It's dark and frightening out there."

"Look at yourself in the mirror! You're scared, can't you see? You're already as large as a proper dragon. It's time to start hunting for your own food."

"I've tried, but the prey fights back," Hydragon complained.

"What did you expect? That someone would offer themselves to you as a free lunch?"

"Davkaleon, nobody has trained me. I'm a poor, miserable orphan. All alone. And there's no one to feel sorry for me. You promised to teach me how to hunt, but you never did. You never have time. I could die, and no one would shed a tear for me. And Heather would miss me. What would she do all day by herself? You're never here, but I'll entertain her with cards, tell her stories about Daeya. And about you! Oh, how I've praised you to her! She already knows that you are the best of the best." He paused. "You're welcome," he added.

"Fine, take some money, buy yourself some lunch, and don't forget to bring some for us," Davkaleon waved his hand dismissively.

"Why does everyone call you Davkaleon? You told me your name was Alfreydon," Heather asked as soon as Hydragon closed the door behind him.

"Alfreydon is my secret name," Davkaleon smiled. "Only a select few know about it. And your secret name is Flower."

"Flower?" Heather questioned. "No one has ever called me Flower before."

"They will, soon enough. Tiger and Aconit told me about it."

"How do you know Tiger and Aconit?"

"We crossed paths by chance once," Davkaleon smiled mysteriously. "Do you know how I can reach you from Daeya?"

"Are we in Daeya? Where is it?" Heather's expression betrayed her confusion. Heather had never heard of Daeya, so she had no idea how to get from Daeya to Attl or Twierks.

"And how did you end up in Daeya?" Davkaleon inquired.

"By accident. You see, I'm not a very good student, and I got confused with the Mage's Clock. I probably calculated the formula incorrectly, and the arrows were not set the right way," Heather sighed. "I'm not very good with formulas, especially when it's necessary to cast spells during them."

"I know what you mean!" Davkaleon exclaimed. "I can't

stand formulas myself. And girls don't need them at all! Dancing, singing, sweet-talking! That's what everyone expects from girls. Formulas are nothing but wrinkles!" In this regard, Davkaleon fully agreed with the etiquette teacher, Mr. Pusik. "Why was the Difeserant chasing you?" Davkaleon asked.

"It all started at the mage tournament," Heather began to explain.

Davkaleon's eyes lit up with curiosity. What the young apprentice of priestesses was telling sounded more than fantastic. It turned out that during the tournament, the mages had inadvertently transported several spectators to different unexpected places. Heather found herself in the domain where the mage Prann grew his gems, guarded by monstrous dinosaurs. Frightened, Heather began to ask the goddess ISIDA for help. The goddess answered her prayers and sent Alfreydon.

"Me?" Davkaleon exclaimed, breaking into a smile.

"Yes," Heather said, nodding. "Whenever I was in danger, the goddess always sent you to me."

Davkaleon's smile grew even wider.

Next, the goddess returned Heather to the rest of the spectators at the tournament. However, the mage Prann was convinced that mage Kovording had orchestrated Alfreydon's appearance in his gem domain to uncover the secrets of his stones, and thus he accused Alfreydon of being sent by Kovording to blind the dinosaur guards.

"Did Kovording send me to blind the dinosaurs?" Davkaleon was genuinely astonished.

"That's what mage Prann claimed. But it's not true, is

it? My goddess sent you, not Prann?" Heather asked.

"I don't know if your goddess sent me, but what I do know is that neither Prann, nor Kovording, nor any other mage sent me to search for stones or ordered me to fight dinosaur monsters. I was seeking a way to you myself and even begged the Fountain of Dreams for us to meet," Davkaleon explained.

"Really?" Heather's eyes lit up with joy.

"And then it emerged that someone had erased the events using an unregistered key," Heather continued. "And not just any key, but the highest key possible. The kind that only members of the Wizarding Council possess. If they had used a lower key, the mages could have easily traced the culprit and scrutinized everything in the records. However, with the discovery of an unregistered high key, suspicions were raised. The mages speculated that someone intended to meddle in the upcoming Twierks tournament; otherwise, why erase the events? The mages couldn't directly confront the members of the Wizarding Council; it would be akin to soldiers demanding answers from their general. Hence, they sought to reach out to you to uncover the mastermind behind it all."

"Davkaleon listened with increasing surprise. He had heard about the keys before from his Adoleeseet friend, Chapius, but he had never been particularly interested in them. On the contrary, he even urged Chapius to talk faster about the keys, which he deemed useless from his perspective. Now, however, his perspective had changed.

"The Mages saw you, me, and the dinosaurs. They were certain that you and I were conversing, and they wanted to discover your identity. That's why the mage Prann sent his Defeserant."

At this, Davkaleon grew alarmed. He himself could easily handle any monster, dinosaur, or Defeserant. But Heather? How would she manage? "How did you escape from the Difeserant?" Davkaleon asked.

"With the help of a Mage's Clock," Heather replied. "The Priestess Mistletoe set the hands on the Clock. All I had to do was think of a single word to myself in case of danger, and the Clock would transport me back an hour to the temple. However, when you appeared on your Aleurh, coming from several different directions, someone tampered with the hands on the Clock. I found myself in a temple, but not the one I intended to be in."

"Did I appear on the Aleurh?" Davkaleon was amazed. "Where?"

"By the fountain near the temple."

Heather continued her story. "Now I must find the Mages' Clock and go back. Ideally, I'll return to the time set by the priestess Mistletoe on the Clock. I remember the position of all the hands, so I can reset them. Then I'll have a few minutes to warn Mistletoe that things won't go as planned," Heather concluded.

"Why would you come back?" Davkaleon asked. "I will marry you and protect you from any Difeserants. I'll hire the best dragons to guard you! They'll protect you when I'm not around."

"No, Alfreydon, I can't. It's not because I don't like you, but you can't do anything without the goddess's permission. Dragons cannot protect anyone from the goddess. She will scatter them into dust."

"Can your goddess find you in Daeya too?" Davkaleon wondered.

"Of course! She's a goddess," Heather replied with conviction.

The story about the Mages' Clock intrigued Davkaleon, but for the first time in his life, he found himself hesitant to search for a magical artifact. The thought of finding the Clock meant Heather would disappear. "If we don't find the Clock, will you still be able to come back?" he asked.

"I've heard of the Silver Arrow amulet, but I don't possess it," Heather sighed. "Someone mentioned that the priestesses of ISIDA can dispatch a messenger with a Silver Arrow, but I'm unsure of the process."

Davkaleon grew anxious. If Heather somehow acquired the Silver Arrow and returned, he needed to learn everything about the Mages' Clock beforehand. "Sketch for me what this Clock looks like and share all you know about it," he suggested.

After a few minutes, he held the drawing in his hands, absorbing Heather's narrative. As they conversed, dawn broke, prompting Davkaleon to hasten to his guardhouse.

*****

"Where were the witches going?" Captain Harding addressed the participants of yesterday's raid in Llill.

One day earlier, they had returned to Assa, bringing along the witches from the temple. However, today, the witches had vanished.

"Well, they're witches, so they're scattered," someone

remarked.

"They're scattered," Harding mimicked, "and of course, you had nothing to do with this scattering."

The audience collectively glanced at the ceiling.

"The priests intend to conduct some sort of ritual with the witches tomorrow. Those who aren't associated with the Svargs will be released, so ensure you retrieve all the witches. The ones you helped scatter," Harding added.

Davkaleon harbored suspicions about the priestly ritual. "I should consult with Dallilla," he decided. Dallilla was one of Davkaleon's father's wives. She was from Llill, and all of Davkaleon's relatives considered her a witch.

Chapter 12. Dallilla

"This is Heather," Davkaleon said to Dallilla. "She says she's never been a witch." Among the captive witches, there are many who claim that they ended up in the temple by accident and are not actually witches. The priests have announced that they will perform an identification ritual tomorrow. Those who pass it will be released and will not face persecution. Do you know anything about this ritual? Is it dangerous for Heather to undergo it?"

Davkaleon turned to Heather and explained: "Dallilla is a witch herself. My apologies, not a witch, but a sorceress. No one touches her because she is my father's wife, and he is a priest. If anyone knows whether this ritual is safe, it's her."

"Do you want me to perform a ritual and determine if Heather is a witch?" Dallilla asked.

"Whether Heather is a witch or not is intriguing, but that's not the main concern. I want to understand the nature of this ritual and whether it poses any danger to her."

"Would you like to undergo this ritual?" Dallilla asked, turning to the girl.

"I'm not sure what kind of ritual it is. Will it be painful?" Heather asked.

"No, it's painless. I just need a drop of your blood."

Heather extended her hand. Dallilla lit several candles and arranged them in a semicircle in front of the mirror. Placing an object in the center, she pricked Heather's hand with a silver pin. A drop of blood dripped onto the object placed within the semicircle. Simultaneously, tiny silvery splashes shot up and swirled within the candle-lit semicircle.

"The amulet of the goddess ISIDA," Heather smiled, "I have one."

The girl handed over her amulet.

"Where did you get this amulet?" Dallilla asked.

"I am a student of the priestesses of the goddess ISIDA. All the students have such amulets," the girl replied.

"You're not from Daeya. Where are you from?" Dallilla inquired.

"I'm from Attl."

"Who were your parents?" Dallilla pressed further.

"I was raised in the family of the priest of Attl," the girl replied, "but I do not know who my biological parents were. I was placed in the priest's family right after birth, accompanied by a note claiming that I was a gift from the gods."

Dallilla nodded to Davkaleon, gesturing for him to follow her into another room.

"What will you do if the girl turns out to be a witch?" Dallilla inquired.

"I'll conceal her, ensuring she doesn't fall into the hands of the priests," Davkaleon responded.

"Do you fancy her?" Dallilla smiled.

Davkaleon nodded.

"Aren't you worried about getting involved with a witch?" Dallilla chuckled.

"So what if she is a witch? My father lives with you, and he's perfectly fine," Davkaleon replied.

"Then hide her and keep her away from the priestly ritual. I'm not sure which land she's from or which family she was taken from, but she carries the blood of sorcerers."

Davkaleon shrugged. "A witch is a witch. No big deal. It might even be advantageous in my line of work. She can speak to the blood, heal wounds, and she's pleasing to the eye."

"Is there anything else you need?" Dallilla asked, noticing Davkaleon's reluctance to leave.

Davkaleon hesitated. "I've heard of a magical potion that ignites love."

"It does exist. But why do you require it? The girl is already smitten with you," Dallilla replied.

"Dallilla, I truly need it! You see, she keeps thinking about returning home. How will I find her then? She's not from Daeya, and she ended up here accidentally. I don't know the way to her, and she doesn't know the way to Daeya. I need this potion to make her stop even considering going back."

"Well, then, slip it into her drink," Dallilla suggested, handing Davkaleon a small vial.

"Dallilla, you always come through for me!" Davkaleon exclaimed happily.

"Wait, it works best with ambrosia juice. I'll give some to you now."

*****

"Are you certain Dallilla wasn't mistaken?" Heather couldn't believe the outcome of the ritual.

"I've never had any association with witches. They were present in Attl, but I never engaged with them. Later, I became an apprentice to the priestesses of ISIDA, but ISIDA is a goddess, not a witch."

*****

Myco's amulet flashed a warning golden light, but Heather didn't notice it as she listened to Davkaleon's tale about Daeya. Raising the sparkling drink to her lips, Heather was interrupted by the iridescent sound emanating from Myco's pendant. She withdrew the glass, watching as the amulet shimmered with golden hues. Bringing the glass closer, she heard the cautious tone of the amulet once more.

"Is there a love potion in the glass?" she asked in confusion, unable to believe what she was seeing.

"Heather, I don't want you to vanish," Davkaleon exclaimed, his voice filled with concern.

"If a messenger bearing a Silver Arrow is sent for you, how will I ever find you? I can't bear to lose you."

"A love potion won't protect me from a Silver Arrow," Heather objected. "If I resist, the Arrow will stupefy me. While a love potion might make me think of you, it won't ensure our reunion."

"What can ensure our meeting?" Davkaleon inquired.

"I'm not entirely certain," Heather responded, "but based on what we've learned, the closest possibility is the Ritual of Intertwined Destinies. It compels those subjected to it to reunite repeatedly, even if they are separated by great distances and different lands." Heather explained.

"Fantastic! That's exactly what we need! So that we can meet again if the Silver Arrow takes you away from me.

Perform this ritual! Right now!" Davkaleon demanded.

"Right now?" Heather seemed a stunned, but after a moment of contemplation, she added, "Why not? It's rather intriguing. I like the idea! Though, I can't say I remember all the ingredients and their exact quantities. There are quite a few."

"Use what you recall! And if you're unsure about the amounts, just add more!" Davkaleon advised.

"Very well," Heather agreed. "After all, following the recipe exactly would be rather dull!"

*****

"I see they share the same mindset," Adamant *chuckled.*

"Of course, she was modeled after him. Why would she need a universal-scale mega-brain?" Ecktoral replied.

*****

"Tiger and I once concocted a surprise drink," Heather recalled. "We had no idea what would happen. The result was a Cheerful Syrup that everyone loved."

Heather removed Myco's pendant and, pressing a turquoise stone, slid it to the side. "Do we have ambrosia juice?" she asked. "I can mix it with anything, but it's best with ambrosia juice."

"We do!" Davkaleon replied eagerly. "Dallilla gave it to me."

Heather began casting a spell. From beneath the blue, pink, and green gems, a magical potion flowed into the ambrosia juice.

"Now, what next? Verbena or datura?" Heather

pondered.

"Add both, just to be sure!" Davkaleon recommended.

"Excellent! I agree," Heather said, nodding. Verbena, veselka, datura, and henbane were added to the ambrosia juice. "Well, that seems to be everything," Heather said, surveying her creation. "Now, I need 40 candles. Do you have 40 candles?"

Davkaleon opened a box of candles. "We do!" he declared joyfully after a moment.

"We need to arrange them in a circle around us," Heather instructed. "And we have to add a drop of our blood to the ambrosia juice."

Without hesitation, Davkaleon pricked himself with a dagger, his curiosity piqued.

"Now I'm going to cast a spell," Heather announced, and she, too, pricked herself with a dagger. In a matter of minutes, everything was prepared. "Oh, ISIDA, the great, grant me strength if I've overlooked something! There are 140 ingredients here! How am I supposed to remember them all?" Heather appealed to her goddess as she took a sip from her glass.

"I'm next!" Davkaleon insisted, intercepting the glass. A buzzing sensation filled his head, and golden bunnies danced across the ceiling.

"Leave it to me," Heather smiled, reclaiming the glass containing the remnants of her creation.

"Let's incorporate Dallilla's potion here, so you won't forget me at your school if the Silver Arrow steals you away," Davkaleon suggested.

"It wouldn't be fair to subject only me to a love potion,"

Heather shook her head, downing the remaining contents of the glass. Her head buzzed, but her heart brimmed with joy. Any lingering worries about her fate seemed to vanish into the distance, and the earlier anxiety regarding the love spell melted away. She felt an urge to dance, reminiscent of the euphoria she experienced at school balls after indulging in Cheerful Syrup.

"A love spell just for me alone isn't fair! But if you're interested, I could create love spells for both of us. See, there are countless untouched stones in Myco's amulet. Myco is my potions brewing teacher, and this section of the amulet is dedicated to love spells." Heather displayed her amulet adorned with hundreds of colorful gems.

"Let's do it!" Davkaleon agreed eagerly.

"Then I should start by explaining love spells, as there are many different kinds," Heather continued. "Myco taught us that if falling in love is solely due to a potion, it won't lead to anything good. But if people already harbor feelings for each other without the aid of spells, a love potion can transform their lives into a fairy tale."

"That sounds like us!" Davkaleon exclaimed. "What else did Myco say?"

"Close your eyes, and I'll recount what I remember from those lessons," Heather said, taking Davkaleon's hand. Together, they immersed themselves in the teachings of Myco's lesson on love spells, culminating in a task to concoct potions.

"The depository will provide you with all the ingredients except those needed for the final section, as it is impossible to dispel such spells," Myco finally said.

"I want the love potion from this last section!" Davkaleon exclaimed eagerly.

"I've never prepared them before," Heather cautioned.

"Of course not! Who would you have made them for before?! But now you have me! So, prepare them now for both of us!" They both drank the potion simultaneously, and a feeling of euphoria washed over them.

"Do you believe in fairy tales?" Davkaleon inquired.

"Yes, indeed!" Heather replied enthusiastically. "My favorite fairy tale is about Ventus and Amans. They fell in love with each other, and their love lasted forever. I'll show you this fairy tale." Before Davkaleon's eyes, a real spectacle unfolded. "I used to believe that Amans was the strongest and bravest of all people," Heather remarked, "but that was before I witnessed your battle with the dinosaur."

Davkaleon had *never* felt so elated. Heather unreservedly regarded him as a hero. There was no ulterior motive, no sense of competition, as often occurred at his school. It was like paradise, only even better.

"Show me your life at your school," Davkaleon requested.

Images materialized before Davkaleon. Heather looked beautiful in her dance lesson; he admired it. "Do you want a laugh? I'll show you how we were taught to dance," Heather suggested with a smile. The scene was genuinely amusing. Heather sat in etiquette class with her fellow students, sticks clenched between their teeth. The instructors taught the girls to maintain impeccable smiles. Initially, it seemed easy. However, their enjoyment was short-lived. The teacher placed small boards on their heads and instructed them to dance. The girls were told that this would help improve their posture. Initially manageable, the task became increasingly difficult as small bowls filled with water were added to the boards. Despite their efforts to move cautiously, the girls struggled to prevent the water from spilling and to keep the sticks in their teeth. When the music accelerated, and the girls spun faster, water spilled from the bowls, screams ensued, and chopsticks clattered to the floor. The once radiant smiles vanished from the faces of the young priestess students.

Davkaleon burst into laughter. "Show me more," he requested.

Heather displayed images of the ball with the students of mages. At that moment, Davkaleon felt a twinge of jealousy. "Do you have any interest in any of the mages or their students?" he inquired.

"Not particularly. Those who study under the mage Kovording are alright, but the students of mage Prann are too arrogant and troublesome."

A warm sensation washed over Davkaleon. Then, Heather showed him the tournament of mage's students. "Let me see your school," Heather said.

Davkaleon became anxious. What Heather had shown him was intriguing. What could he show her about his school life in return? Training with swords and spears? Or his time spent in the guardhouse? She wouldn't find that interesting. After showing Heather some pictures from school, Davkaleon decided to recount the Adoleeseet

Chapa incident. He showed her how he saved the little boy.

"Oh, you're so kind!" He caught Heather's thought, and he felt a sense of fulfillment blossom within him. Davkaleon then shared memories of a trip to the temple in the rock and their first encounter.

"You remember everything so vividly," Heather remarked.

"Of course! Chapa and I revisited the temple and made a copy of the recording. You're in that copy. I rewatch it a lot," Davkaleon explained.

"Really?" Heather's eyes sparkled with joy.

Next, Davkaleon recounted the initiation scene and the encounter with the Dragon of Adolees. Heather gasped in fear as she witnessed the battle with the monsters. Then came Walpurgis Night, and Davkaleon showed Heather how he tried to find her, narrating how Gragbrag's black cat chased Heather's white kitten, and how he threw sapphire earrings onto the stage.

"These are my favorite earrings! I knew it was you who threw them to me. You appeared for just a moment and then disappeared," Heather exclaimed.

"Yes, the temple banished me because of the confrontation with Gragbrag, but I tried to find you afterward," Davkaleon revealed.

Their brief encounters flashed through their memories.

"Could you repeat what you thought of me? It is *so* good," Heather requested, closing her eyes.

These were Davkaleon's reflections at the temple of Arragorra during last year's Holy Thanksgiving Week. On this occasion, it was customary to express gratitude to the gods and loved ones, and Davkaleon had included Heather in the circle of his beloved. "Last year, just before the Holy Thanksgiving Week feast, I found myself in battle, and you saved me. I heard your voice urging me to turn back. If I hadn't, I would have been struck by a spear," Davkaleon recounted.

Heather recalled the vision that had flashed in the crystal ball.

"That was the first time I saw you without a mask, even if only for a moment. Then you vanished, but since then, you've become my talisman," Davkaleon said.

"Oh, how touching. Did I really help you?" Heather was deeply moved.

Davkaleon nodded. "And why did your priestess, Mistletoe, set the hands on the Clock of the Mages so that you would encounter a Difeserant?" he asked. "It's perilous."

"That was my exam assignment. I was supposed to handle the Difeserant, but I failed," Heather explained.

"Your assignment?! Are they out of their minds at your school? How could they assign such tasks to girls? You could have been killed!" Davkaleon exclaimed, his indignation evident.

"I had a magic amulet with me. It was supposed to help me overcome the Difeserant, but I failed," Heather said sadly. "Now the main concern is not getting expelled from school."

"On the contrary! Let them expel you! You'll be safe and well with me. You know what a good husband I'll be to you," Davkaleon insisted.

"Davkaleon, I always knew you were like this. I often imagined our meeting. You're speaking just the way I've always dreamed of hearing. But I need to return to school and learn how to defeat the Difeserant, then the students of the mages, and finally the mages themselves; otherwise, a very sad fate awaits me."

"Why?"

"The priestess of Vesta told me that I would be played as a trophy at the Twierks tournament." Heather softly sang a verse from the song she had heard from the priestess of Vesta during the fortune telling.

The priestess Vesta gave me warning
About changes in my life
At parting I have heard exhorting
You'll not return to native Attl

Your way's to far-off Arragorra,
To place where stone Alatar
I see the long and distant road
Through flame and ice to afar star

What means this strange fantastic picture?
Events completely of the whack
Effects and causes make huge mixture
Time River turns its passage back

The Twierks will play the wheel of Fortune,
Two armies fighting at sunrise
The tourney loser learns misfortune
For winner you become a prize.

"When I announced that I would change my fate, the priestess said that all I needed to do was take part in the tournament myself, defeat the Twierks mages, and win the tournament."

"She is a vile instigator! Let her go to these tournaments herself if she's so smart. And you should be with me; I'll protect you from everything! Tournaments are more in my line!"

"No, Davkaleon, she is not an instigator. She said it sarcastically and advised me to learn good manners in Miss Loveliness's lessons."

"As for the tournament, do not be afraid, I will take part in it, and I will win, and I will not give you up to anyone," Davkaleon said.

"I've heard you say that to me many times in my dreams," Heather smiled, "but I want to be the mistress of my own destiny." And if that means participating in a tournament, I'll do it."

*****

"Stop, stop, stop. I like this. Is that what you planned?" Adamant asked.

"I didn't plan those words exactly, but they are very much what I anticipated. When I tasked Mage Eximi with shaping the character of a girl, I envisioned her exactly like this. I didn't want her to be a pronounced leader. Two leaders will never get along well together, but she shouldn't be an obedient, quiet person either. It's tedious with the quiet ones; they get bored quickly," replied Ecktoral.

Davkaleon was slightly stunned by Heather's words. It went against everything he was accustomed to. That wasn't the way things were done in Daeya. In Daeya, a man had to fight, win battles, and a woman had a completely different role — to provide warmth, comfort, but not to rush into participating in tournaments.

Heather sensed Davkaleon's doubts. Still, she smiled and said, "And most of all, I would like us to be in this tournament together."

"This is much better!" Davkaleon smiled. "But you don't have to fight! Casting spells, attracting luck — that's your role. You're my talisman, Heather. Stay as the talisman. Talismans do not fight; they inspire. Do you know how empowered I felt when I saw the concern for me in your eyes? I was ready to face the entire army alone!"

"You don't have to face the whole army alone. I don't want to lose you! As for the tournament, you might not be around. I need to learn all these witchcraft tricks and be able to defend myself. And besides, I like it, it's interesting," Heather smiled, "and if you're around, then it's not scary at all."

After a short silence, Heather asked: "Davkaleon, are you already a mage or are you an apprentice?"

"I'm still studying," Davkaleon said.

He didn't want to admit that he had nothing to do with magic. Although, maybe that wasn't entirely true. Chapius claimed that there was no magic at all, only science. And even though he hadn't yet become a novice student, he would surely become one. True, he performed tasks with the help of Elfid, but what difference did it make? The main thing was that he accomplished them.

They exchanged memories for a long time. In the morning, when Hydragon opened the door, he saw Davkaleon and Heather sleeping at the table, holding hands.

Chapter 13. The Feast of Holy Thanksgiving

A few days later, the feast of Holy Thanksgiving was held, so the priests ceased all persecution of the Llill witches. Davkaleon took Heather to the festival, eager to show her the best side of Daeya. Music filled the air, merchants competed to offer their goods, and street actors entertained the crowds. Davkaleon, Heather, and Aleurh sat at a table adorned with Daeya's snacks and drinks.

"What's that?" Heather asked, pointing to a blazing dish being wheeled between the rows of tables on a cart.

"It's a dragon's favorite dish," Aleurh smiled. "You should try it. It's very tasty."

They enjoyed the performances, sampled Aleurh's favorite dish, and strolled through the center of Assa. Fortunately, the weather was fabulous, a rare occurrence in Daeya.

"Why didn't you bring your witch to the priestly ritual?" someone asked.

Davkaleon turned abruptly. Krasius Pompeus, Pompedides, and several others approached him and Heather, their dragons accompanying them.

"Protect her!" Davkaleon shouted to Aleurh and, swiftly grabbing a fan of knives from his pocket, hurled them at the enemy dragons, aiming for their mouths. A dragon wounded in the mouth cannot spew flames, thus reducing the threat to him and Heather. Meanwhile, someone from behind was preparing to throw a spear at Davkaleon.

"Look back!" Heather screamed at the top of her lungs.

Reacting quickly, Davkaleon jumped back and, drawing a pair of swords, charged towards Pompeus.

"Are you attacking officers, you brute?" Pompeus roared in response, drawing his sword, and engaging in battle.

Davkaleon had no doubt that he could fend off Pompeus and the others, but he worried whether Aleurh could protect Heather and handle the enemy dragons simultaneously. Three of the dragons already had their mouths injured, which would make it easier for Aleurh. However, one fully combat-ready dragon remained, and it charged towards Aleurh. Suddenly, the enemy dragon stopped abruptly, closed its eyes, and shook its head.

Heather watched the scene in surprise. Davkaleon's boldness captivated her, but why did it all feel so familiar? Had she seen this before? Yes, she had! In a vision within a crystal ball during her test at the ISIDA school! She had thrown sand into a dragon's eyes, stopping it in its tracks. And then she had done the same to another dragon. That was it! The other dragon also stopped and closed its eyes! This realization meant that it would be easier for Davkaleon and Aleurh.

Davkaleon fought like a lion, determined to swiftly dispatch the enemies and aid Aleurh.

The battle didn't last long. Guards poured out from the temple.

"Bloodshed on the holy Thanksgiving holiday!" the priest exclaimed indignantly. "I will immediately send a message to the school authorities." A wide smile spread across Krasius Pompeus's face. "And to your superiors in the army," the priest added.

"Why blame us? He attacked us!" Pompeus protested.

"And what did you expect? That I would stand by while

someone insults my girlfriend?" Davkaleon retorted, his indignation evident.

"No one insulted your witch!" Pompeus declared.

Davkaleon gripped his sword once more, but the priest intervened, preventing him from using it.

"Where in Daeya is it acceptable for a well-mannered officer to refer to a woman as a witch?" the priest asked coldly.

"Dear Mr. Priest," Heather spoke in a gentle voice, "allow us to present gifts to the temple on this sacred holiday. That was our original intention in visiting the temple."

"Gifts to the temple?" the priest inquired, his tone softening slightly. "You may present whatever gifts you wish to the temple, but that won't absolve your companion from facing a court martial for assaulting officers," Krasius interjected.

"Of course not," Heather replied calmly. "Could you please inform me of the location for the trial? I will need to provide testimony about the incident, including how you referred to me as a witch and how Davkaleon single-handedly managed to handle the four of you and your dragons."

At Heather's words, Pompeus turned visibly pale.

"That's correct!" Davkaleon chimed in, his delight evident. "You four have received education from a reputable school! How can you turn out to be such incompetent fools? You're not officers, but feeble incompetents!"

"Oh, you insolent brute!" Pompeius exploded.

"Double the gifts," Heather smiled, handing the priest a handful of gold coins.

"And from me and my dragon, too," Davkaleon added, pulling out his wallet.

"Very well, and from us as well," said the shamed adversaries.

"Dear Mr. Priest," Heather cooed, "show kindness on this holy holiday. There's no need to involve the school or the army authorities in what transpired."

"Aren't you afraid?" Davkaleon asked as they walked away from the temple.

"When I'm with you, I fear nothing," Heather replied, smiling.

Davkaleon beamed in return.

"Is there a Cliff Rock in Daeya too?" Heather inquired as Davkaleon mentioned they would be going ashore.

"First, there will be entertainment on the shore, and in the evening, there will be a fireworks display over the Rock," Davkaleon explained.

"This Cliff Rock looks exactly like the one in Attl," Heather remarked.

Cliff Rock in Attl? Davkaleon recalled reading about it in the notes of the jeweler Piromis. Could Heather be from the same Attl as the jeweler?

"Do you know about the Tartar?" Davkaleon queried.

"Yes, it's an undercurrent near Cliff Rock. They say there's also an underwater waterfall named Tartar, but no one has actually seen it," Heather responded.

It appeared that Heather was indeed from the Attl that the jeweler had written about.

"Have you heard of Piromis?" Davkaleon inquired.

"Yes, there's a shop belonging to the jeweler Piromis in Attl. It's located right on the square in front of the temple. Are you referring to him? How do you know about Piromis? Does Daeya have his shop too?" Heather asked, surprised.

"No, there's no Piromis shop in Daeya. However, the jeweler left behind manuscripts in which he talked about Attl and magical jewelry. I've read the first three manuscripts. Do these drawings mean anything to you?" Davkaleon asked as he sketched symbols from the jeweler's manuscripts. He remembered them well.

512   4913   5832

"The first sign is the temple of the Serpent god, the second one is the Eye of the Gods in the city of Gods, but ordinary mortals can't get there," Heather explained.

"The temple of the Serpent god? Are you sure?" Davkaleon was amazed. "In Daeya, this drawing marked the temple of Stall, but this temple was destroyed a long time ago."

"I've never heard the name Stall, but the Serpent god has many names; maybe Stall is one of them," Heather suggested.

"Maybe. Do you know anything about the number 2519?"

"We have been taught about this number in the lessons of sacred mathematics. They explained to us that this number is associated with planets, and if you want to get to this planet, you need to dial the appropriate number on the Mage's Clock. I don't understand why. Of all of us, only Tiger figured out this number to the end, but she studied astronomy before she got to the ISIDA school."

Davkaleon perked up. Even Elfid couldn't find anything about the number 2519 in his manuscripts, and Heather, it turns out, knew the secret of the number.

"Tell me," Davkaleon demanded.

"This number is often used by mages to quickly move from one place to another. It was explained to us that this is due to the unusual properties of the number. If you try to divide 2519 by any number from 2 to 10, you will fail. But if you subtract from 2519 a number that is one less than the number you want to divide it by, then you will always succeed."

Heather drew a table.

Number	Subtract	Divide by
2519	1	2
2519	2	3
2519	3	4
2519	4	5
2519	5	6
2519	6	7
2519	7	8
2519	8	9
2519	9	10

"You see, the number in the third column is always one more than the number you need to subtract from 2519."

Davkaleon saw it was true.

"We are required to remember the results of the division because they are used in the formulas of transitions in the Clock of Mages, but I have not yet memorized them all. If you want, you can calculate them yourself."

Davkaleon pretended that he would enthusiastically perform any calculations.

"I do not know why the number 2519 is in the circle, but the next sign is the symbol of Attl. I have one," Heather said, and took out a pendant on a chain.

"The penultimate symbol is the famous Bible of Attl library."

Heather had never seen the last symbol, the three dots in the circle, but if the penultimate sign marked the library, then the last sign had to be associated either with the manuscript numbers or with their storage location.

Heather didn't know what the numbers 512, 4913, 5832 under the drawing meant. However, it didn't matter so far. The main thing is that Davkaleon learned that 2519 in the circle means the transition from the city of the gods to Attl. However, neither Davkaleon nor Heather knew why the number was in the circle.

"Heather, do you know if it is possible to get to the city of the Gods not from the temple of the Serpent god, but from somewhere else?"

Heather didn't know that. The music started playing, and they went dancing. The first few dances flew by

161

unnoticed.

*****

"Come on, finish this nirvana," Adamant chuckled.

"Ai-ya-yai, Adamant, what a bad villain you are. You want to take the candy away from the boy," smiled Ecktoral.

"He's had enough of euphoria. You gave him a girl, and she explained the formulas of transitions in the Clock of Mages. Let him strain his own brains," Adamant did not concede.

"Eximi! Ecktoral called out, "arrange the messenger with the Silver Arrow!"

The face of the mage Eximi appeared in front of Adamant and Ecktoral. Looking at Heather and Davkaleon, and assessing what was happening at a glance, the mage Efingo de Eximi declared: "I listen and obey, my lord."

*****

"Oh," Heather shuddered and pressed her hand to her eyes. "There are some images flickering in front of my eyes," she said, then paused.

"It's all gone now," Heather smiled and held out her hand.

They resumed dancing. Suddenly, Heather froze and pressed her hand to her eyes again. "What's wrong with me?" she asked, confused. "Everything is swirling before my eyes." Then, an expression of amazement appeared on her face as she began to look somewhere behind Davkaleon.

Davkaleon turned around to see a short, skinny guy behind him, showing something to Heather. Davkaleon wanted to push him away but remembered that it wasn't worth starting a fight during the Holy Thanksgiving holidays. Instead, he simply growled at the short man to leave. Davkaleon had never seen him before, but the short guy addressed him by name and said: "Dear Davkaleon, it's not that I'm not happy to see you. I just didn't have time to miss you."

Davkaleon was taken aback by such audacity. Then the short guy grabbed Heather by the arm, and fleeting images flashed before Davkaleon's eyes. He saw Heather with the diminutive figure, far ahead near the Rock cliff. Davkaleon immediately sprinted after them. Just moments ago, he had been experiencing the greatest bliss, but now he was consumed with rage. He reached the cliff in haste. The short man and Heather stood precariously close to the edge.

"Hey, you lunatic!" Davkaleon shouted. "If you have any sense left, release Heather, and I won't harm you!"

Ignoring his plea, the short man held Heather tightly and leaped off the cliff into the roaring ocean below. Davkaleon raced to the edge. Waves surged beneath him. He plunged into the turbulent waters of the Tartar waterfall. Within moments, the waterfall carried him to the depths below. But there was no sign of Heather and the short guy. Davkaleon ascended, meticulously scanning his surroundings. Could the short man have passed through the waterfall? Davkaleon dove again and again, exploring every nook and crevice, but alas, Heather had vanished.

This was the darkest day of his life.

Once ashore, Davkaleon trudged to the nearest bar and ordered the strongest ale available. After downing his fifth or sixth mug, it dawned on him that the short man was likely dead, but did he care? As for Heather, she was a witch. And if anyone had a chance to survive a leap from the Rock cliff, it was her. There were rumors about the witches of Llill, tales of their ability to endure where any strong, healthy Daeyan man would have perished long ago. Heather may not have identified as a witch, but that didn't negate her potential. Perhaps she was unaware of her own powers. Dallilla had explicitly mentioned that Heather had witch blood in her, and Heather worshipped the goddess ISIDA, like all Llill witches. She was undoubtedly a witch. "Not just a witch, but a sorceress," Davkaleon corrected himself, then shrugged. Oh, what did it matter? Whether witch or sorceress, all he wished for was her survival.

Davkaleon began to think about what the short man had shown Heather. By the gods, it was a tiny silver arrow! Heather had once mentioned that the priestesses of ISIDA could dispatch a messenger with a silver arrow. That's it! That explained everything! That's why Heather had gone with the short man, appearing bewildered. It seemed she didn't comprehend her own actions. With this realization, Davkaleon ordered another large pint, downed it quickly, and then set off for Elfid.

He found his brother engrossed in ancient manuscripts.

"Have you come across anything about the Mages'

Clock?" Davkaleon inquired, recounting Heather's tale of her sudden appearance in Daeya.

"I've stumbled upon the name, but I'm not familiar with their workings," Elfid replied.

"Elfid! You're a lifesaver! Where can I locate this Clock?"

"In the Temple's Depository, most likely."

"Heather mentioned that I appeared riding Aleurh, with five identical copies of each of us manifesting simultaneously. How is that possible?"

"I can't fathom how to assist you with this," Elfid shrugged, "the simple trick with mirrors that I devised for you and Chapa a few years back won't suffice here. They'd detect it immediately, no matter where you aimed to go."

"God help them if there are five copies. One of me is plenty," Davkaleon waved his hand dismissively.

Chapter 14. Davkaleon and Mathematics

"Heather spoke of the significance of the number 2519. But she didn't know why this number was within the circle," Davkaleon lamented.

"Let's crunch the numbers and see what transpires," Elfid proposed.

Number	Subtract	Divide in	Result
2519	1	2	1259
2519	2	3	839
2519	3	4	629
2519	4	5	503
2519	5	6	419
2519	6	7	359
2519	7	8	314
2519	8	9	279
2519	9	10	251

"Look at the seventh line, where you subtract 7 and divide by 8."

"I look, but I can't find any reference to a circle," Davkaleon replied.

"The number 314 is related to the circle," Elfid tried to explain. "Actually, it's 3.14, not 314, but apparently the clockmakers didn't include the decimal point."

Elfid took his time to explain the connection of 314 or 3.14 with the circle. At the military school where Davkaleon studied, they didn't bother with the precision of circle calculations. You just took the diameter and multiply it by 3.

Do you really need more precision? Why? Well, if it's absolutely necessary, the teacher of arithmetic told students to multiply not by 3, but by 3.1 or by 3.2. Elfid's insistence that the diameter should be multiplied by 3.14 was difficult for Davkaleon to grasp.

"Okay, I believe you," Davkaleon waved his hand. "So what should I do when I reach 2519 on the circle? Should I click on 7? Or 8? Or 314?"

"I can't answer that," Elfid sighed. "Most likely, you'll need to find a clue on the spot."

"Look at this!" Davkaleon exclaimed, delighted. He drew from memory the last symbol and numbers from the note found in the Pillantelli cave.

512   4913   5832

"Now look at the numbers of the first three manuscripts."

826   5072   6097

Davkaleon was obviously proud of himself as he said: "If you add 314 to the number from the note, you'll get the number of the manuscript!"

$$512 + 314 = 826$$

"Now, let's try with the next number," Davkaleon offered enthusiastically.

He quickly drew a table.

Numbers	First	Second	Third
From the note	512	4913	5832
From the manuscripts	826	5072	6097
Difference	314	159	265

Davkaleon looked at the result with disappointment. He expected the number to match that of the second manuscript. Unfortunately, that wasn't the case.

$$4913 + 314 = 5227$$

The number of the second manuscript was 5072, and Davkaleon received 5227.

"It would be too easy if mages set simple tasks," Elfid smiled.

"Do you know how to get the number of the second manuscript?" Davkaleon asked Elfid.

"Yes, I know. I even know how to get the number of the third manuscript. The problem is that I do not know what the fourth number should be. At our school, the ratio of the circumference to the diameter is calculated with great accuracy, but even this accuracy is not sufficient. This ratio was initially considered equal to 3, as in your school. Then it was considered equal to 22/7. If you divide the circumference by the diameter, you get 3.14285714."

He shook his head before continuing.

"The first three digits are 3.14. They will allow you to calculate the number of the first manuscript, but the next three digits will result in an incorrect number for the second manuscript.

More recently, scientific circles in Daeya have believed that the fraction 355/113 gives an absolutely accurate value. It is equal to 3.14159292. If you use this fraction, you will get the correct numbers for the first and second manuscripts, but not the third.

In our day, by far the most accurate value of the ratio of the circumference to the diameter is the fraction 103993/33102. It is equal to 3.14159265. If you use 3.14159265, you will get the correct numbers for all three manuscripts. But I'm not at all sure that this will work for the fourth manuscript; moreover, I doubt it.

And it's not even a matter of calculating the ratio of the circumference to the diameter even more accurately. The ratio can be calculated, but it's better to involve Chapius. He is an Adoleeseet, and science is much more developed in Adolees than in Daeya, so it will not be difficult for him to find out what we need.

The problem is that we don't know which number to add the next three digits to."

"Why don't we know?" Davkaleon didn't understand.

Elfid drew a table.

"Do you see the big bold question mark?" "The numbers from the note, 512, 4913, and 5832, probably represent some kind of sequence, but I can't figure out which one."

Numbers from the note	3.14159265	Sum	Numbers from the manuscripts
512	314	512 + 314 = 826	826
4913	159	4913 + 159 = 5072	5072
5832	265	5832 + 265 = 6097	6097
?	Ask Chapius	?	?

"After talking with Elfid, Davkaleon contacted Chapius. "Do you want to walk to the temple in the rock?"

Chapius was always ready for such adventure. "And you didn't show her to me?" protested Chapius when Davkaleon told him about Heather.

"I would have shown you in time if she hadn't disappeared," Davkaleon sighed.

Chapter 15. A Trip to the Temple

The next day, after classes, Davkaleon returned to his room. Upon closing the door, he couldn't help but exclaim in amazement. Four Aleurh jumped out from the four corners, each with a rider who bore a striking resemblance to Davkaleon.

"Chapius!" Davkaleon guessed. "And who might this be?"

"The Chapa-shka sisters," the three sisters laughed, assuming their normal Adoleeseet appearance.

"Dvina, Mlava, and Bilda," Chapius introduced his sisters.

"Sign the contract," Dvina said, holding out the paper.

"Which one?" Davkaleon was taken aback.

"An ordinary one, in which you promise to marry the three of us," Bilda burst out laughing. "And don't you dare cheat on us. We are jealous girls."

Davkaleon was rendered speechless!

"Don't scare my friend," Chapius intervened. "He's a brave guy, but not that brave."

"Is this a joke?" Davkaleon asked hopefully.

"What kind of joke? A contract is a serious matter. Family life is the same. If you behave yourself, we won't even roast you. Maybe just a little bit for fun," Mlava said, exhaling a small flame toward the ceiling.

"Don't make promises. Husband's roast is my favorite dish," Dvina intervened. "I tell my hubby that during each of our quarrels."

"Don't be too scared, they're just joking," Chapius

laughed. "Sign the contract and consider yourself the luckiest guy in the world."

"What's in the contract?" Davkaleon persisted.

"Well, you're persistent," the older sister said. "We've been practicing impersonating you with your dragon all evening, and you don't thank us at all. Do you know how hard it is to grow a dragon's muzzle on my waist?!"

Davkaleon unfolded the contract.

"A music and dance promoter? And what on earth is this?"

"Not what, but who. It's you. Our brother told us that you're always on the move. That's exactly what we need. You see, we make a living performing on stage. You once attended our performance, but there are more music and dance groups in Adolees than drops of water in the rain. The competition is fierce. We love singing and dancing, but we also need to earn a living. And you travel all over the world; you've been to all the surrounding countries, and now you want to get to your witch in Twie…"

"*Stop, stop, stop!*" Chapius shouted. He recalled that the word 'Twierks' was forbidden in Daeya.

"Oh, you can't mention that word in *your* Daeya," Dvina waved her hand.

"I told them about our adventures in the temple and how the mages' students offered you an excursion to the 'Tender Monster' during Walpurgis Night. So, my sisters got the idea to sign a contract with this Monster."

"A music and dance contract with the *Tender Monster*? And where do I fit in? I don't play the balalaika, and I'm not a trumpet player either. If I start singing, all the visitors of the *Monster* will run away. Who will pay your sisters?"

"Davkaleon, you don't need to sing or dance. The girls want you to say a few warm words about their performances while visiting the *Tender Monster*."

"And what if I don't make it to the *Monster*?"

"You'll get there; you're quite determined. Chapius told us all about you," the younger Bilda grinned.

"If I do get the chance to visit the *Tender Monster*, I'll talk about you without needing a contract."

"You can't do it without a contract," Chapius insisted. "How else will you take them to the temple in the rock? The temple will refuse them entry. Everything must be arranged with the contract. They've been pestering me to take them with me for a long time, so I've spent many days in the Depository figuring out how to make it happen. Your three years are up, and the temple must let you in. As for them, you'll present an official contract."

"Besides, you'll receive our 10%," added Dvina. "It's stipulated in the contract."

"What on earth is this role called?" Davkaleon asked, giving in.

"The promoter. Music and dance. Don't forget it."

"Put 50% in the contract. The temple will never believe I agreed to less."

*****

They journeyed to the temple on the eve of the Lughnasadh Night.

"Since when did the disciple of the Mage of Twierks

become a lowly promoter?" the temple rumbled indignantly.

"Since the Great Dragon of Adolees personally welcomed me into the guild of Fire-Breathing Dragons," Dveena declared, proudly tossing her head.

"Prove it," demanded the temple.

Dveena hesitated for a moment, but when she spotted Telatr, she immediately approached it. An image of a DRAGON materialized in the air.

"Today, upon the request of my general, I accept his granddaughter Dveena into the guild of Fire-breathing Dragons. Those admitted into the guild must demonstrate their commitment to serving Adolees by engaging in combat. Dveena, show us your skills!" the DRAGON commanded.

A battle scene unfolded. After observing Dveena's prowess for a few minutes, the temple graciously conceded that they could proceed to the *Tender Monster*.

"Will the esteemed Lord of Twierks enlighten us on this matter?" Chapius inquired in his most courteous tone.

The temple hesitated momentarily. On one hand, it appreciated being addressed as the Lord of Twierks, but on the other hand—what sort of fool wouldn't know such basic things?

"Very well, it's not often that the Great Dragon of Adolees personally inducts someone into the Fire-Breathing guild. Hence, I shall dispatch you to the *Tender Monster*, but don't anticipate a gentle journey," the temple declared.

They were whisked away, tossed, and turned as if their

limbs were being pulled in different directions. It felt as though their heads had detached and were observing their bodies' flight from a distance. Upon arriving in the foyer of a building, Davkaleon checked his arms, legs, and, of course, his head, just to be sure everything was intact. All seemed to be in order. The foyer transformed into a vast hall with tables and chairs. The jovial company had barely settled around a large oak table when a waiter swiftly approached them.

"First and foremost, I require a weapon," Davkaleon demanded.

The temple only permitted an adamantine dagger to be carried inside, leaving Davkaleon feeling ill-equipped without his usual array of swords and knives. Chapius and his sisters, however, seemed unfazed; if they required a weapon, they would simply grow one.

"Steel? Adamant?" the waiter inquired promptly.

"Adamant!" Davkaleon exclaimed, elated by his stroke of luck. Acquiring adamant weapons in Daeya was nearly impossible, though he braced himself for the staggering price.

"I'm a promoter," Davkaleon stated following the purchase. "Who oversees entertainment here?"

"And what, pray tell, are you promoting?" the waiter mocked.

"Not *what*, but *who*," Dveena declared, her tone firm. "And don't you dare ridicule the protege of the Great DRAGON himself."

With those words, Dveena transformed into a dragon, seizing the waiter and exhaling flames towards the ceiling.

She then juggled the waiter, or rather, the dragon's paw did, before gently lowering him to the ground. Shifting back into her human form, she sang a tender verse, her demeanor transformed from fierce to gentle in an instant.

"It might work," remarked a furry representative of the Tender Monster, who appeared seemingly out of thin air. "It will require, of course, a bit more fire, a bit more emotion, but that's not a problem."

"They can present a ready-made performance, brimming with fire and emotion," Davkaleon declared, remembering his role as a promoter.

Shaggy nodded, and the Chapa-shka sisters promptly transformed the hall into a vast stage. However, they didn't have to exert themselves; the tables and chairs vanished of their own accord. It would be inaccurate to describe the sisters' performance as anything less than captivating. Davkaleon watched the fiery dance with delight. At times, the dancers resembled beautiful maidens, yet they were not quite so, as their number of limbs didn't always tally up to two and two; it was in a perpetual state of flux. Hair color and length also underwent constant changes, all of it twisting, intertwining, and flashing with flames in time with the music. If the furry representative sought fire and emotion, then he was sure to be satisfied.

"On the night of Lughnasad, everyone will be at the carnival. The following day, people will be resting, and then the day after, you can present your performance," the shaggy man said, nodding.

"We require an advance payment," Davkaleon insisted.

"Ha! You'll get over it! The *Tender Monster* never pays anyone in advance; he always demands advance from others," the shaggy individual retorted.

"As part of the advance, we request access to the Mages' Clock, and in return, we offer a 50% discount on our fee," Davkaleon proposed.

"That's a fair offer," the shaggy man swiftly agreed.

The Mages' Clock materialized beside Davkaleon. Just a few days prior, Heather had sketched it for him and explained several of its scales and hands.

"Come here," Davkaleon beckoned to his companions and adjusted the hands on the clock as Heather had instructed.

*****

Four identical dragons with identical riders appeared from four directions. The fifth descended from above. Davkaleon spotted Heather near the fountain, accompanied by a Difeserant.

"Where is your Abal-Dural?" the Difeserant growled.

Someone tampered with the Clock of the Mages. A black haze engulfed everything. Davkaleon was whisked away and carried to an unknown location. An unseen force hurled him to the ground. Glancing around, Davkaleon recognized the grove near Assa. Heather was nowhere to be found. Chapius, his sisters, and Aleurh were also missing.

"What's happening? They're trapped in Twierks by my doing and won't even be able to return! I need to hire a dragon to take me to the temple in rock," he thought, but then a doubt crept in. "Will the temple open its doors for me and allow me into Twierks?" Another thought crossed his mind, "It's better to rush to Elfid for counsel first, and then hire a dragon."

His brother always offered sound advice.

"If only he were home, if only he hadn't gone anywhere," Davkaleon muttered to himself, setting off towards Elfid.

"It's a relief to see you alive," Elfid rejoiced upon sighting Davkaleon. "Chapius got in touch with me and filled me in on everything."

"Are they all safe?" Davkaleon asked anxiously, his worry dissipating upon hearing the affirmative response. He vowed to offer gifts to the gods in gratitude.

"Where are they now?" he inquired further.

"They're at the *Tender Monster*. They received payment for the performance by the Chapa-shka sisters. They were even promised transportation back using a Mage's Clock, but until they exhaust their funds, they're in no hurry to return. It seems they're quite enjoying themselves there."

*****

"Davkaleon may be distressed about Heather's disappearance, but the question is how far he's willing to go to find her," Adamant remarked. "His attempted trip to Twierks doesn't necessarily indicate his commitment; he was attempting to go there without her."

"I'll instruct Mage Eximi to make the necessary preparations, and then we'll see," Ecktoral replied.

"Davkaleon enjoys a good fight, so tasks involving combat won't reveal much. However, he lacks patience and isn't keen on studying, especially during competitions

where he anticipates winning first place. Let your mage devise something along those lines," Adamant suggested.

"Well, Adamant, you're quite the sadist. You seem intent on burying a lovelorn man behind textbooks, especially at a time when he's grappling with such mental turmoil," Ecktoral quipped, grinning.

"What did you expect? That I'd arrange a couple of paradise houris in front of him as consolation? You think his feelings for Heather are so strong that by using her as bait, you'll manipulate him into doing whatever you need during the tournament. Let's see. Studying instead of engaging in sports is unpleasant, but it's not a death sentence. Will he comply? Or will he rationalize that if not Heather, then another girl will always come along, and he can't afford to skip the competitions?"

"Alright, let's see," Ecktoral agreed, and after summoning Mage Eximi, provided him with instructions.

"Now we can look at Heather's return," Adamant remarked, reclining in his chair.

The ISIDA school materialized on the screen.

*****

"Is she back? Are you alright?" Priestess Mistletoe inquired, her gaze fixed on Heather, who had just reappeared.

For the first few minutes, Heather looked around, clearly disoriented and not fully comprehending her surroundings.

"Oh, what was that? It felt like I met... How strange? I can't recall who I met," Heather expressed, her confusion evident. Her recent memory had disappeared!

Chapter 16. The World Institute of Technology of Changing History

"Have they explained to you what WITCH means? Who's to say what it is?"

"A sorceress," Aconit offered her interpretation.

The questioner looked at her in surprise. "A sorceress?" Do you think you will become a witch because of practicing witchcraft?

"Perhaps not witchcraft, but maybe magic or sorcery," Aconit suggested. It appeared that the new name was starting to have a positive effect on her, and the former Iya's natural timidity faded away.

"Is that what you were told? Miss Loveliness, have you explained to the students what WITCH means?" the questioner inquired.

"Of course," Miss Loveliness replied, "Lala explained."

"Lala! Have you explained to the students what WITCH means?"

"Indeed," Lala affirmed, "Loveliness clarified."

"Lala! Do you think about anything other than your 60-25-60? Or did you volunteer to help to sell your witch's potion?"

"Do not exaggerate," Lala frowned. "It's only 50-25-50."

Waving his hand in the direction of Loveliness and Lala, the man introduced himself: "My name is Monsieur Marquis Mage Efingo de Eximi."

"Wow, that's long," Tiger whispered.

"I am the creator of the WITCH technology," continued

Monsieur Mage Marquis.

"WITCH is an acronym for the *World Institute of Technology of Changing History.* The WITCH technology has nothing to do with any sorcery, witchcraft, or enchantment. Everything here is based on science."

Monsieur Efingo de Eximi proudly looked around the classroom, with the students. It was evident that he was expecting applause and exclamations of admiration. When they didn't come, he looked around the classroom once more, this time with undisguised surprise. "I hope you understand well what you are going to participate in? You will be in the thick of the most important events. It will depend on you whether entire countries, epochs, or even planets will survive or perish."

"And what are we supposed to do?" Tiger asked.

"Your actions will be different every time. Sometimes you will have to go to the place and take part in events; and sometimes you can do Twierksing without leaving home."

"What does *Twierksing* mean?" Aconit asked, while the other girls nodded their heads in unison to show support.

"Don't you know that either?" The mage Eximi was taken aback. "Lala! Did you tell them what the word Twierks means?"

"Twierks? Don't they know?" Lala was surprised in her turn.

"Lala, they have just finished the initial level. At the initial level, you are not supposed to know this. Okay, you can go, I'll explain myself."

"Well, it's always like that. They can't really tell what they expect from me, and then they're also unhappy," Lala complained resentfully, heading for the exit.

"At the initial level, it has already been explained to you that Twierks was created by the will of those who became members of Twierks' Council. Rules and everyday life supported by mages of Twierks."

"And who are these members of Twierks' Council?" Tiger asked.

"You will learn it on the next level. For now, we will talk about Twierks," answered Mage Eximi. "The name Twierks was not chosen by chance; it is also an acronym. It stands for **T**echnology of **W**orld **I**ntelligent **E**xchange of **R**ealities **K**its and **S**amples. You may think of Twierks as Tools for Worldwide Exchange of Realities. You create Reality in one place and time and move it to another. My WITCH technology makes it easier. Very often you don't need to leave Twierks for this. That's why we call it *Twierksing.*"

"Why do we need to do such exchange?" Another student, Zlata, asked.

"And what happens with that place where Reality was created after you move it to another place?" Tiger inquired.

"It depends on various factors, but, Tiger, you are ahead of time," Mage Eximi answered.

Maya, another student, interrupted. "Tiger, don't behave like a child. It depends on who was making this Twierksing. If it was made by our tender Zlata, then 10

182

copies of each Reality would appear to ensure that nobody perishes. If Twierksing was performed by somebody from Mage Prann's school – well, it would be good if at least somebody survives."

"Reality Exchange does not work exactly like this, Maya," Mage Eximi commented without diving into details. The girls listened, holding their breath. This was all very intriguing, but also very alarming.

"I received a task from Twierks' Council to develop WITCH technology, and I obtained the Council's permission to select those who would work with this technology. I chose ISIDA's school because I like its education and consider it the best in Twierks. I selected you and brought you to this school from different parts of the world. I pay for your education and ensure that you are completely prepared for the future job," Mage Eximi continued.

"What about students of Mage schools? Do they also work with this technology?" asked Heather.

"Yes, they do. I mean the best students of the best Mage schools. I've already told you what the word WITCH means. Now I'm going to tell you about the word 'mage' because it is a generalized term. There are three levels of mages in Twierks, and the name of each level is also an acronym."

"Magus is the first level, which stands for Material Advanced Generator of Urgent Situation.

"Mage is the second level. That stands for Material Advanced Generator of Events.

Magee is the third level. That stands for Material Advanced Generator of Events Exchange."

He spoke slowly to give the students a chance to process the information. "Creating urgent situations such as volcanic eruptions, comets, or earthquakes is much easier than orchestrating smoothly flowing events, as you don't have to worry too much about integrating what happened before and after the emergency event. The most difficult task is substitution of seamlessly flowing events. The mages and witches of Twierks specialize in this. You have been bestowed with the greatest honor of being trained to become Twierks' witches."

The girls felt that the revelation by Mage Eximi would change their entire lives. However, there was so much information that they were confused (and totally silent, not knowing what to ask).

"You now have higher access to your twierky; read about Twierks there," Marquis Eximi suggested. "Now everyone except Heather can leave."

As soon as the other girls left the classroom, Eximi told Heather, "You're going to high school."

"Now? What about my vacation? I haven't seen my family for almost a year; I miss them," Heather exclaimed, clearly upset.

"Don't worry," Eximi reassured her. "You know that time flows differently everywhere. You can always return to Attl in time."

Heather sighed, realizing it was futile to argue.

"The high school is named the School of Mixed Time," Eximi continued. "You will frequently return to Twierks to continue your studies here. At the School of Mixed Time, you'll learn ordinary science, and at the School of the Priestesses of the Goddess ISIDA, you'll delve into magical sciences. It will be beneficial for you to integrate both sets of knowledge, understanding how science intertwines with magic."

"How will I know when to return to Twierks? And how will I get back?" Heather asked anxiously.

"You will do this with the help of the Twierks' amulet," Mage Eximi replied, handing her the amulet. "Your twierky will guide you on how to use it." He nodded towards the opposite wall. "Enter this door, and you will find yourself in a secret cave."

Heather turned her head to where the mage pointed. She could have sworn that there was no door there just a moment ago.

"Think the words 'School of Mixed Time'," Eximi continued, "and there will be an exit in the cave. You will emerge from the cave and find yourself in a glade with a stream. There's a path near the stream that will lead you to the hill. Beneath it, there's a building surrounded by a fence. Enter there. That's the School of Mixed Time. At the entrance, they'll ask for documents – here they are," the mage handed over the package and continued, "Here's an explanation of where to go and who to contact. You'll need to find Mr. Quantrell Frost's office. Hand him this letter." An envelope appeared in Heather's hands. "Tell him that the Goddess ISIDA sent you and that you are a now student of the priestesses of the great goddess."

Chapter 17. The Clock of Mages

Sitting on a rock, Davkaleon and Chapius rubbed their bruised spots. The temple had ejected them.

"You are an idiot! Stupid! Blockhead!" These were some of the epithets the temple didn't hold back on when it became apparent that Davkaleon still didn't know how to reach Twierks.

"How could you have apprenticed to a Twierks mage?" The temple was perplexed.

They had arrived in Llill just a few hours earlier, entered the temple, and headed to the Depository. They even found a plethora of information about Twierks. The Depository graciously provided them with numerous instructions for accessing Twierks. However, they were missing the final piece to gain entry: a key, or at least a password. Davkaleon and Chapius had even meticulously transcribed excerpts from the Depository's instructions.

The first method for entering Twierks involved special access points, provided you were at the right place and time. How do you determine the correct location and timing? It's simple! You need to consult the witch-net, wizard-net, or any other available Twierks network. What? You don't have access to any of these networks? Then this method isn't suitable for *you*.

The second method involved personal keys. These seemed to be the same keys Chapius had mentioned, but they were of such high level that Davkaleon and Chapius couldn't rely on obtaining them anytime soon.

The third method required knowledge of a password. According to the Depository's instructions, one must go to the Twierks entrance and whisper the password to himself. Davkaleon knew the entry point; ever since his first visit to the temple, he remembered seeing the sign of the golden rose and the curled dragon. However, neither Davkaleon nor Chapius knew the password. They attempted to guess and experiment for so long that the temple eventually couldn't tolerate it and ejected them.

"We should have left the password alone and asked the Depository about the Mages' Clock!" Davkaleon exclaimed, slapping his forehead.

"The temple surely won't permit us into the Depository today," Chapius sighed.

"Come on, let's give it a try," Davkaleon insisted.

"When you learn how to enter Twierks, I'll open the door for you," the temple retorted.

"But I won't attempt to enter Twierks today," Davkaleon attempted to negotiate with the temple. He tried to sound reasonable. Logical. But, after all, he was Davkaleon.

"Are you arguing again?" the temple's tone grew stern.

Fearing being permanently ejected from the temple, Davkaleon sadly trudged away.

"Didn't work out?" Aleurh asked. The dragon waited for them on the rock.

Davkaleon shook his head sorrowfully. However, as he made his way back to Assa, his spirits lifted. "I know where we can find the Mages' Clock! How did I not think of it before? Aleurh, let's stop by the Carducci magic shop."

Davkaleon thought about the dragon's tale about the Carducci shop and the rumors that swirled around it. A few years earlier, one of the dragons at the Dragon Tavern in Assa had explained how those who ventured into the shop might vanish, while those who never entered would emerge unscathed. Davkaleon had been here once before. Just like last time, the merchant wore a crimson cape adorned with golden embroidery. A golden hoop adorned with red and green stones held his long hair in place. Jars, stones, jewelry, purses, amulets, swords, knives, and numerous other objects, the purposes of which Davkaleon couldn't fathom, cluttered shelves, lay on the floor, and hung from the ceiling. From somewhere within the shop, there came croaking, quacking, mooing, and hissing. The interior of the shop seemed much larger than its exterior. Davkaleon approached the merchant and inquired about the Mages' Clock.

"Do you have a million sickles?" The merchant eyed Davkaleon with interest.

"A million?" Davkaleon was taken aback by the sum mentioned.

"How much did you expect?" The merchant chuckled.

"I don't have that amount at the moment, but I'll obtain it," Davkaleon replied confidently.

"You can gather a million sickles? I welcome such clients. What's your name?" the merchant inquired.

"Are you the one who visited Adolees and the Pillantelli Cave?" the merchant continued after Davkaleon identified himself. "Did you engage in an arbitration court with goblins a few years ago over a note from the jeweler Piromis?" the merchant clarified.

Davkaleon nodded.

The merchant scrutinized Davkaleon intently and asked, "Would you consider taking a loan from bankers?" then added, "They'll likely grant it to you." After a brief pause, the merchant waved his hand. "Never mind the bankers. I'll extend a loan myself. Return tomorrow, and I'll draft a contract," the merchant offered.

"Will you sell me a Mages' Clock?" Davkaleon asked eagerly.

"Sell?!" The merchant burst into laughter, laughing so hard that tears welled in his eyes. "Do you want to buy a Clock of Mages for a million sickles?"

"What's so funny about that?" Davkaleon asked, puzzled.

"A million is the price for a *one-time use* of the Clock. There isn't enough money in all of Daeya to buy it," the seller explained.

"But you bought it here in Daeya. So, there must be enough money," Davkaleon countered.

"Did I buy it? Me? No, of course not. Only mages of the highest rank can afford to own a Magie's Clock."

"Then what do you want a million for?" Davkaleon inquired.

"I have information about when and where the passage to the Clock will open," the seller replied.

Davkaleon paused for a moment, certain that there was a Clock of Mages in the Temple in the Rock. If he hadn't been a complete idiot and, instead of trying to guess the password, had asked for the Mages' Clock in the Depository, he might have gained access to it for free. But he didn't, and the temple threw him out. What now? If he refused the deal, he wouldn't gain entry to Twierks or to the manuscripts of the jeweler Piromis in Attl anytime soon.

As for Heather, he probably wouldn't see her again. There might be hope with Twierks that he could find his way there someday in the future, but no such hope with Heather. Heather said she was 15 years old. In Daeya, at that age, they marry off girls. In Attl? Probably the same. With Heather's beauty, there would be countless suitors. If he found a way to her in a couple of years, she'll be someone's wife already.

Even if Heather tried to persuade her parents or her goddess to delay her marriage and explained that she's met a guy who genuinely wanted to marry her and was about to arrive with rich gifts and a full purse, how convincing would her story be? The prospective groom lives in Daeya, yet neither Heather herself nor her mysterious fiancé knows how to travel between Attl and Daeya. When he met her, he said his name was Alfreydon, but everyone in Daeya called him Davkaleon. How favorably would Heather's parents receive the request to postpone her marriage until the appearance of the unknown Alfreydon-Davkaleon?

His choice was obvious. "Prepare your contract. I'll come to you tomorrow!" Davkaleon declared.

*****

"Where do you intend to go with the Clock?" the seller inquired the next day.

"To various places," Davkaleon replied vaguely,

avoiding discussion of Twierks or Attl.

"Does that include Attl?" the seller pressed.

Davkaleon looked surprised. "I do plan to visit Attl," he admitted.

"Jeweler Piromis has crafted numerous magical jewels. I desire them all. If you manage to acquire at least one of his jewels for me each time, then your use of the Mages' Clock will be free. However, if you return empty-handed, you'll owe me a million."

"But each of Piromis's magical jewels is worth far more than a million," Davkaleon protested. "Furthermore, I'll have to cover the cost of using the Mages' Clock to return."

"I will pay you for the jewelry. My aim is to have you in my employ consistently, which is why I'm offering you a trial expedition. It will be free for you, even if you're unsuccessful on your first attempt."

"What if the manuscripts are destroyed or hidden?" Davkaleon asked.

"As I mentioned, your first use of the Clock will be free. If you locate and peruse the jeweler's manuscripts, and then obtain the jewelry, I'll cover your expenses and pay for the jewelry."

"I need instructions on how to use the Mages' Clock," Davkaleon insisted.

"You will receive them, but bear in mind, I've read them and they're quite complex. If they were straightforward, my terms would be different."

"I understand."

"Then sign the contract." Davkaleon scanned the parchment and signed it. The seller smiled. "I'll inform you when the passage to the Mages' Clock becomes accessible," he said.

"Why can't you inform me now?" Davkaleon queried, surprised.

"Because I don't currently know. Take the time to study the instructions. Perhaps you'll glean some insight in the meantime."

Chapter 18. An Unexpected Journey

The owner of Carducci shop was correct about the instructions. Some aspects were clear, but Davkaleon had never encountered many of the terms before. This was despite Heather telling him what she knew about the Clock of the Mages. But inscriptions such as Ecliptic Longitude, Galactic Latitude, Celestial Meridian, Elongation, Ephemeris, and others equally puzzled him.

"Alright, I know how to find Heather, and I'll figure out the rest as I go," Davkaleon thought.

A knock on the window interrupted his thoughts. A raven was circling outside the glass, holding a note in its beak.

"The passage to the Clock will open at dawn," Davkaleon read aloud.

"The passage will appear with the first ray of the sun," explained the master of the Carducci shop. "Once you're in front of the Clock, you'll encounter numerous panels. Most of them are sliding, and within them, you'll find panels leading to the next level. It's crucial for me that you eventually locate the treasures of the jeweler Piromis, but this time, I'd be pleased if you could at least find one of the following manuscripts of the jeweler."

"Have you ever used the Mages' Clock yourself?" Davkaleon inquired.

"Yes, but I no longer wish to," replied the shopkeeper at Carducci's.

"How did you return?"

"I memorized the combination that was set on the Clock before I made any changes. Most of the time, it worked as expected, but on one occasion, I found myself somewhere completely unexpected. By some miracle, I survived and managed to return. This might not scare you, as you came seeking the Mages' Clock of your own accord. I doubt you're expecting an easy journey."

"I'm accustomed to danger," Davkaleon shrugged. "What else do you know about the Clock that could assist me?"

"Perhaps nothing more. Aside from the fact that this journey is free for you, I'll give you another gift. Not just one, but two. Firstly, I'll give you this pendant. It will serve as your translator."

The shopkeeper extended the pendant.

"And secondly, I'll give you the amulet that kept me alive when I couldn't return the first time."

The shopkeeper produced a ring adorned with a dark ruby and offered it to Davkaleon.

"Press lightly on the back of the ring with your thumb," instructed the shopkeeper.

Davkaleon complied and jumped back in surprise as his doppelganger materialized next to him.

"Push harder," the shopkeeper advised.

Davkaleon applied more pressure, causing the doppelganger to bounce a few meters away.

"Now, swipe your finger right, left, up, down," the shopkeeper continued to give instructions.

The doppelganger obediently followed the commands it received.

"Now, ease off the pressure."

The doppelganger drew closer.

"Reach out and touch him."

Davkaleon extended his hand, which passed effortlessly through the doppelganger.

"As you understand, the doppelganger won't fight on your behalf, but he can distract your pursuers if they appear, giving you a few minutes to slip away."

"Thank you, this is an incredible gift," Davkaleon exclaimed with delight.

"That's not all. Go to the mirror and press the ring," instructed Carducci.

Davkaleon complied and gasped in surprise. As soon as his doppelganger appeared in the mirror, he himself disappeared. "Wow!" Davkaleon cried.

"Impressive, isn't it?" Carducci smiled. "By the way, doors and walls are no obstacle for an incorporeal doppelganger. That's so you can be in the room yourself while your doppelganger is somewhere outside the door."

Davkaleon nodded in understanding.

"Keep in mind that using the doppelganger for more than 15 minutes continuously is risky. The doppelganger operates at the expense of your energy, and if you expend too much energy, you'll become exhausted."

Carducci scrutinized Davkaleon carefully and added, "You're a strong guy, perhaps you could manage 20-25 minutes, but that's pushing the limit."

Davkaleon once again gazed admiringly at the ring with the dark ruby stone.

"Now, to the point. I know the contents of the note from the Pillantelli cave."

The shopkeeper placed a copy of the note from the cave

in front of Davkaleon.

512   4913   5832

Carducci continued. "The Temple of Stall has been destroyed, so it seems that there is no way to reach the Eye of the Gods from Daeya. However, I noticed the next sign, 2519, inscribed within the circle on the Clock of the Mages. I'm uncertain how to interpret it. I'll transport you to this sign, after which you'll continue the journey alone."

Davkaleon wanted to clarify something else, but the ringing of bells interrupted him, and a passage appeared in the wall. Davkaleon and Carducci proceeded forward. A door materialized at the end of the corridor. Carducci placed his hand on it, and the door opened noiselessly. Directly opposite the door was a huge mechanism with many arrows, tables, scales, and symbols. Some of the arrows were motionless and others moved. The ones which moved did so at different speeds. On the other wall, there were many recorders drawing obscure figures and signs. Davkaleon glanced at the third wall only briefly. Some flowers and hearts were on it.

Carducci went to the opposite wall and pulled apart the neighboring drawings. He repeated this procedure several times, and Davkaleon saw the familiar drawing of 2519 in a circle.

Carducci pressed it, and a ledge with numeric buttons

appeared under the drawing.

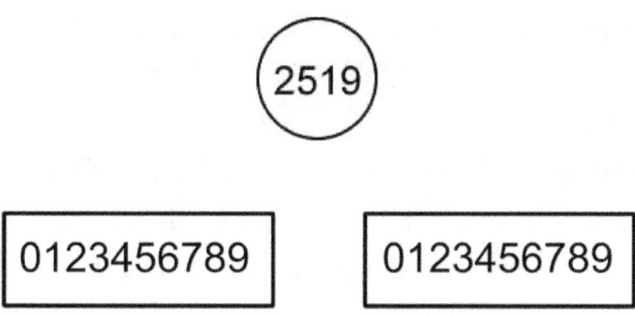

"Do you know what to do with it?" Carducci asked.

Davkaleon shook his head. He didn't want to reveal what he had learned from Heather and Elfid.

"Well, I'll leave you to wonder what to do."

With that, Carducci left the room, leaving Davkaleon alone. He was about to search for the right panel to set the Mages' Clocks as Heather had told him when an idea struck him. He decided to first journey to Attl, locate the manuscripts—or better yet, the jeweler's creations themselves—and then proceed to find Heather at her school. Glancing at the buttons, Davkaleon pondered his next move."

"It seems that it was like this...you need to subtract 7 and divide by 8," Davkaleon remembered and clicked on the corresponding numbers."

In the next moment, something changed. The number 2519 in the circle was still on the panel of the Mages' Clock, but the ledge with the buttons had disappeared. The Clock Room looked a little different. He must have moved somewhere.

"I need to find out whether it's Attl or not. And if it's

Attl, then get to the library. Maybe I'll get lucky and find the manuscripts," Davkaleon thought.

He opened the door and stepped out into the corridor. It was clearly a different corridor. It branched, turned, and branched again.

"I won't even find a room with a Mages' Clock like that," Davkaleon thought. "I need to go back and draw a plan of the maze of corridors so that I can return later.

He turned back and began to search in his pockets for a piece of parchment or leather. There were many items in his spacious pockets. He had already walked quite a long way back when he heard a voice. Davkaleon stopped and listened. The gifted translator amulet accurately conveyed the nearby words.

"There's no better time to get rid of him. To think that the son of a slave girl became the Highest Priest of Attl is incomprehensible to my mind."

"How did he get recognized by the gods?" the second voice asked.

"I've been talking to the Chief Invisible. He is convinced that the High Mage of the Temple set it up with the help of his mirror. This mirror was hanging in the office of the previous Highest Priest all the time. In the last years of his reign, the previous Highest Priest, in my opinion, did not make a single decision without the advice of a mirror," the first voice answered.

"What does the Chief Invisible advice?"

"Get rid of the damn Tot-tze-Attl, of course."

"That's understandable. But how? Have you seen how many people are gathering for the start of tonight's evening prayer? Everyone is convinced that he was chosen by the gods themselves, and that the gods are waiting for him in the city of the gods today."

"The Chief Invisible is sure that this is a trick, and the High Mage of the Temple is behind this trick. He suggests letting Tot-tze-Attl ascend supposedly to the gods, and when he returns, strike him with lightning. He even promises that everyone will hear the divine speech exposing the son of a slave and declaring punishment for insolence."

"What does he want for this?"

"A return to real sacrifices, as it was in ancient times, instead of slaughtering bulls."

"It's possible. Prisons are full of criminals, why feed them?"

"The Invisible wants more."

"It's problematic. The Attlids won't go with this."

"They can. The Invisible predicts several lean years and a protracted war."

"What is required from us?"

"Acknowledge the divine speech and thank the gods for the enlightenment."

"It's not difficult."

The voices stopped. Davkaleon was about to move forward, but the conversation ahead resumed, and Davkaleon froze in place.

"What do you think about the emeralds of Piromis?"

At these words, Davkaleon started up. Is this really about the same Piromis whose first three manuscripts he read? Or are they talking about his descendants?

"I think there will be a lot of people who want to get them during tonight's evening prayer."

"That's understandable. I'm talking about something else. Piromis delivers offerings to the Temple on every holiday. Among these offerings, there are always emeralds from the jeweler's treasured box. You are the keeper of the Temple's treasures. Let's exchange those emeralds that are in the treasury for those that are stored in the Piromis box."

"How do you envision it? Are we to simply stroll into the treasury, snatch the emeralds, and waltz over to Piromis' shop for all to see?"

"No, of course not. There's a passage from the dungeon of the Temple that leads directly to Piromis' house. It seems the jeweler isn't aware of it himself, but I once observed the High Mage of the Temple utilizing it. That's the passage I intend to use, but I require the emeralds."

"And why do you assume Piromis must possess the Stone of Destiny? He's stashed numerous emeralds in the Temple's treasury. Perhaps the coveted Stone is among them."

"I believe the Stone of Destiny still resides in Piromis's box, because I trust in your intellect. Haven't you ever taken a couple of stones home for the night with each new batch of gifts from the jeweler, made a cherished wish, only to wake up the next morning and discover it hadn't come true? And if you're still not the Highest Priest, then it didn't come true."

Davkaleon listened with growing astonishment as a pair of priests deliberated over the logistics of swapping out emeralds.

"The simplest approach would be to swap out the entire box with its contents," suggested one.

"Wouldn't that be considered theft?" voiced the other, with concern. "You know, pilfering treasures from the Temple is to court unprecedented trouble."

"What sort of theft would this be? We'll return as many emeralds as we took."

"Do you have a suitable box?"

"Yes, indeed. I have one. I ordered the same one from the jeweler Benvenudi."

From the ensuing conversation, Davkaleon gleaned that the jeweler Piromis possessed a stock of emeralds, among which one is believed to be the Stone of Destiny. However, nobody, including Piromis himself, knows which emerald holds this coveted status. All these stones are housed in a box, purportedly bestowed either upon the current Piromis or his ancestor by the High Mage of the Temple.

"And why doesn't Piromis himself know which of his emeralds is the Stone of Destiny?" Davkaleon pondered. "Or perhaps he does know but chooses not to disclose it in order to sustain his emerald trade? What a lucrative business!"

While the priests continued their discussion, they finalized their plan to exchange emeralds and proceeded towards the Temple's treasury. Davkaleon trailed behind them silently, keeping a safe distance. As the priests approached the imposing door, Davkaleon pressed the gifted ring with all his strength, hoping his doppelganger would remain distant enough to avoid detection, and then slipped in behind the Attl's priests. The treasury of the Temple was breathtaking. Davkaleon had never beheld such an abundance of gold, precious stones, and jewelry.

"The emeralds of Piromis are here," Davkaleon overheard.

The priests poured the stones into a sizable box and made their way towards the exit. Davkaleon followed closely behind them, his doppelganger obediently trailing from a distance.

"Stop! Who goes there? Guards! There's an intruder in the Treasure Corridor!"

Davkaleon turned around. The priests ahead also pivoted and caught sight of Davkaleon's doppelganger. They hurried forward, but their agility was clearly lacking, hindered by their priestly robes. Davkaleon could have easily outpaced them, but he was unsure of where to flee. Opting for what seemed most logical, he slowed his pace, allowing the guards to attempt to seize his doppelganger. Presumably, they would be frightened off.

"Varakush!!!" A heart-rending scream pierced the air, causing Davkaleon to instinctively cover his ears. Several guards recoiled in horror from Davkaleon's doppelganger.

The priests dashed ahead, navigating through a maze of corridors and staircases. Davkaleon realized he wouldn't be able to memorize all the twists and turns, so he focused on keeping pace with the priests while ensuring his doppelganger remained distant. Eventually, the priests came to a halt before a blank wall. No windows, doors, or other features adorned the area. One of the priests touched the wall, and suddenly, they found themselves in a small room. Davkaleon looked around in bewilderment. He would have understood if a door had materialized in the wall or a passage had opened for them to enter, but nothing of the sort occurred.

The priests approached a beautiful ornate panel on the wall, adorned with precious stones. "Where are we?" one of them inquired.

"We're in the secret domain of either the High Mage of the Temple or the Highest Priest, or perhaps both of them. Few individuals gain access here. I obtained entry when I joined the Council of Four," the speaker explained.

With a concealed mechanism, the speaker activated the panel, causing it to slide aside, revealing another panel adorned with several symbols. Among them, Davkaleon recognized the symbol from the note found in the Pillantelli cave.

"You can get to Bible-at-Attl from here," the second priest gasped.

"You can get to many places from here, look at how many panels there are, but for now we need the house of Piromis.

Davkaleon took a quick look around. Dozens of different paintings, murals and stained glass decorated the walls. The priest pressed one of the signs on the panel, and they found themselves in a corridor ending in a glass door with five compartments.

"And if they see us?" One of the priests asked.

"They won't. The middle part of the door displays what is happening in the Piromis corridor. The compartments on the left and right depict activities around the corners, one leading to the residential area of the house, and the other to the shop and workshop. The far-right compartment showcases several small booths with drawings and sketches, from which visitors can select their preferences to place an order. Multiple booths are connected by corridors to ensure that visitors entering from another corridor won't attract attention. The far-left compartment housed the shop itself."

There was no one behind the glass doors, and all three of them exited into the corridor. The door closed and vanished.

"Just look, where is it?" One of the priests exclaimed.

"You mean the door? Yes, I know it's disappearing. I haven't figured out the secret of how to open it yet, but it doesn't matter. There's an exit to the park from the house," the second priest explained.

"And if someone is in the house and sees us?"

"There's no one here. Have you forgotten that everyone from all over Attl is gathering for tonight's evening prayer? It's not every day that the gods summon the Highest Priest."

Davkaleon felt dizzy.

I need to get behind the priests in the sketch booths and stop pressing the ring. The 20 minutes that Carducci talked about have long passed, Davkaleon thought. He didn't know if it was an accident, but he straightened his numb fingers.

"What are you doing here?" One of the priests demanded when he saw Davkaleon suddenly appear.

"Davkaleon pressed the ring. His doppelganger instantly rebounded and ended up next to the second priest. He involuntarily extended his hand, but it passed through the doppelganger.

"Varakush!" There was a shrill scream, and the priests rushed out.

"Well, that's even better," Davkaleon thought as he entered the shop.

The first thing that caught his eye was the hide of a huge bull hanging on the wall. The story of the identical emeralds' origin was depicted on the skin. According to the narrative, one of these emeralds was the Stone of Destiny. The description stated that the Mage of the Temple had provided the jeweler Piromis with numerous emeralds, all of which precisely replicated the shape of the coveted stone, along with a box for their safekeeping. It remained unknown which of the stones was the Stone of Destiny, even to the jeweler himself. The tale concluded with the assertion that the High Mage of the Temple had cast a protective spell on the emeralds: if someone were to steal them, they would meet a gruesome fate, and the stolen stones would return to the Mage's box of their own accord.

The bottom line indicated the price of one stone.

"Stealing is not right, and I am not a thief," Davkaleon resolved.

Though he had several gold coins in his pockets, he was unsure of the exchange rate between Daeya's and Attl's coins. Deciding that the cost of one Daeya's gold per stone was more than sufficient, he began his search for a box of emeralds. It proved to be relatively easy. Piromis appeared to trust in the mage's spell and didn't seem overly concerned about guarding the box. Taking some stones from the box, Davkaleon replaced them with a handful of gold coins. It was time to depart from the jeweler's house. As he approached the front door of the shop, he found it closed. Davkaleon then set out to find an exit to the park. Upon leaving the jeweler's house, however, Davkaleon froze in amazement. He had never witnessed such a vast gathering of people. It was a sea of humanity, with no clear focal point. A mountain loomed in the distance, catching Davkaleon's eye. He decided to head toward it, thinking that he might gain a better vantage point from its summit. As he ascended, the aroma of roast lamb grew stronger. It was a fortunate coincidence; Davkaleon was feeling hungry.

Sitting near the summit and savoring a succulent roast lamb, Davkaleon surveyed his surroundings. It was now evident to him why the cross with concentric circles symbolized Attl. The view from atop the mountain, with Attl sprawling below, perfectly mirrored the symbol's design. What had Heather called this mountain? It was something like Attl-ass. Yes, Mount Attl-ass.

The chatter of patrons from the makeshift diner filled the air, accompanied by the aroma of roasting lamb on spits. From their conversations, Davkaleon gathered that the evening prayer would be led by none other than the Highest Priest of Attl, Tot-tze-Attl himself. No one knew what to expect next. All that was certain was that the gods had summoned the Highest Priest, leaving the Attlids curious about Tot-tze-Attl's impending encounter with the divine.

Outside, darkness descended, heralding the imminent appearance of the moon. Heather referred to it as Lit. Interestingly, Daeya also had its own Lit.

"I wonder if it's the same Lit or a different one?" Davkaleon pondered.

Suddenly, all conversation ceased. The Highest Priest had commenced the prayer. A few minutes later, a resounding voice echoed from somewhere above: "Highest Priest of Attl, are you prepared to meet the gods?"

Presumably, the Highest Priest responded with a "Yes," because from the vantage point of Mount Attl-ass, everyone could witness the majestic figure of a man beginning to ascend. The crowd fell silent, transfixed by the spectacle as the Highest Priest ascended toward the gods. Soon, his figure became indiscernible, vanishing completely behind the clouds.

While everyone is preoccupied with contemplation and anticipation, it's an opportune moment to attempt reaching the Bible-at-Attl and then find Heather, Davkaleon thought as he departed from the hospitable open-air snack bar and made his way towards the Temple.

He entered the Temple unimpeded; all eyes were fixed skyward, and nobody spared him a glance. Davkaleon wandered alone through the deserted corridors for quite some time. It was at least an hour before he caught wind of muffled voices emanating from around the next bend. Davkaleon came to a halt.

"The death rays failed during the announcement of the new Highest Priest, and the cursed mages of the Temple spared their lackey. This time, the son of the slave must meet his end. The Chief commanded to infiltrate the secret chambers of the Highest Priest. The Temple mages often lurk there. They will likely employ unexpected measures to shield their puppet once more. Divide into groups of 5-6 Invisible Ones and position yourselves in the corridors leading to the secret chambers. If any mage is headed in that direction, detain them."

"Can I remove this hood? It's hindering my ability to discern what's happening," another voice inquired.

"Absolutely not! Your face must remain concealed," an indignant voice retorted.

The first voice continued issuing instructions. "The Chief also instructed a dozen Invisible Ones to infiltrate the mages' domain."

"How are we supposed to do that?" voices queried. "We lack both the Rod of the Temple mages and the ankh, the symbol of the high priests."

"The Chief entrusted me with the amulet of Prann, which will guide me to the concealed door. Somewhere along this corridor lies the passage to the mages' domain. No matter how minuscule the crack around the door may be, invisible to the naked eye, the amulet will detect it."

The voices fell silent. Davkaleon cautiously advanced a few steps. Around the bend, figures clad in black cloaks with hoods shuffled slowly along the wall. Fifteen to twenty minutes elapsed.

"I've found it!" A triumphant voice exclaimed.

The figures halted. Davkaleon observed as those positioned against the wall attempted to access an invisible door: they pushed, twisted, and traced sacred symbols. For a while, the door resisted, but then the Chief Invisible emerged, pressed an unfamiliar amulet against the wall, and the door yielded. Several figures entered the chamber. Davkaleon pressed the ring with all his might and dashed after them.

"A stranger!!!" Davkaleon heard a loud scream behind him. Immediately after, another voice shouted: "Varakush!" Someone must have attempted to seize Davkaleon's doppelganger, mistaking him for Varakush.

The passage sealed shut, leaving the doppelganger stranded in the corridor outside the door. The black-robed figures inside the room paid no heed to the cries about Varakush. Likely assuming that the Invisible Ones in the corridor would handle Varakush. Davkaleon wasn't certain if this room was the same one leading to the house of the jeweler Piromis. If it was, then there were fewer stained-glass windows and paintings adorning it. On one wall, Davkaleon spotted a familiar ornate panel adorned with precious stones. Several ominous black figures approached it, scrutinizing the stones and delicate scrollwork, but the secret panel remained elusive. As the black figures retreated from the panel, Davkaleon swiftly replicated what the priests had done hours earlier. The panel slid aside, revealing another panel etched with several symbols. If it was indeed the same panel, there were fewer symbols present. The diamond symbol pointing to the house of Piromis had vanished.

"Look, the panel has moved!" someone from the Invisible shouted and rushed toward the panel bearing the symbols.

Chapter 19. Bible-at-Attl

Davkaleon clicked on the symbol for Bible-at-Attl.

In the next moment, he found himself amidst a multitude of papyrus scrolls, parchments, clay tablets, and other unfamiliar items. It was undoubtedly a vast library. As Davkaleon walked among the scrolls and manuscripts, he bitterly realized that without at least an approximate knowledge of their numbers, he wouldn't find the Piromis manuscript. All he could do was locate three of the jeweler's manuscripts with known numbers and confirm they matched the ones he had in Daeya. He did just that. The first and second manuscripts were identical to those his brother had brought him. As for the third manuscript, while the beginning was the same, it was longer, listing artifacts created by the jeweler Piromis.

Davkaleon recalled that when he had examined the third manuscript at home, he had noticed what appeared to be a torn-off piece at the end of the papyrus. Now, he laid eyes on this missing fragment. It contained a list of jewels crafted by a jeweler upon the request of a mage. The first mentioned was the Stone of Destiny, which Davkaleon had read about in the second manuscript. Following it was the amulet of the Black Rose or Dragon

Rose, a tale Davkaleon had encountered in the third manuscript. The list continued with a Ring with a Great Opal, a Ring of Kings, a Serpent Ruby, and seven divine rings.

Delving into his pockets, Davkaleon retrieved a piece of leather and meticulously transcribed the names of the first few artifacts when suddenly, he heard a shout: "A stranger has trespassed into Bible-at-Attl!"

Davkaleon turned his head, spotting a figure clad in a black raincoat emerging in the aisle between the shelves. Casting a quick glance to the other side, he found it deserted. Swiftly stowing his notes in his pocket, Davkaleon also tucked away the open manuscript detailing the jeweler's creations, and drew out a dagger. With a forceful strike, he aimed at the advancing Difeserant. Brown blood splattered onto the floor as the blade found its mark. From the Difeserant's body, several appendages extended, grappling with Davkaleon. He retaliated, severing one of them, only to witness another sprouting in its place. Aware that only fire could subdue a Difeserant, Davkaleon pondered where he could procure it in Bible-at-Attl. As another Invisible One materialized in the passage, followed by yet another, Davkaleon braced himself for the impending confrontation.

Bringing down a shelf of manuscripts onto the Difeserant, Davkaleon dashed towards an open space. Clattering echoed from behind as the Invisibles pursued, limited by the narrow passages. Bible-at-Attl stretched before Davkaleon like an endless maze with no apparent entrance or exit; he had no notion of how to escape.

Darting right, then left, and back to the right, he stumbled upon a hatch concealed in the floor, which sprung open, sending Davkaleon plummeting downward. Stretching out his arms, he grasped at the walls of the vertical tunnel, managing to slow his descent but tearing the skin on his hands in the process. Wedging his limbs against the walls for support, he peered downward into the dimly lit abyss. Whether it led to a stone floor or a well infested with snakes remained unclear. Perhaps he should attempt to climb back up? Though the ascent would prove arduous, he had managed to slow his fall, indicating he might have the strength to climb.

"We need to descend and ensure he's truly finished," a voice from above called out.

"Have you ever witnessed anyone surviving the waterfall of Tartar?" came the sarcastic response from another voice.

"Tartar?" Davkaleon exclaimed to himself, a mixture of delight and tension washing over him. Piromis had mentioned the waterfall of Tartar, and the jeweler wrote about the Cliff Rock. Both landmarks were in Daeyan. As he pondered the jeweler's notes, Davkaleon wondered whether these referred to the same Tartar and Cliff Rock or different ones altogether. Now presented with the opportunity, he felt compelled to investigate. If they were indeed the same, it would validate the training he received from Master Gandall. If not, he dared not dwell on the implications.

Davkaleon lowered his arms and descended swiftly. Within moments, he plunged into the water, feeling the forceful current seize him and sweep him away. Looking upward, he spotted several Difeserants hurtling from above. As he sank deeper, Davkaleon observed the Difeserants metamorphosing into aquatic monsters. Despite his rapid descent, the transformed creatures, now resembling enormous sharks, closed in on their fleeing target. Below, a black funnel emerged, surrounded by swirling white eddies. Davkaleon halted his descent and swam towards the center of the vortex. With the sharks closing in, he dove into the dark void below. Now plummeting into a seemingly endless abyss, Davkaleon found solace in the fact that he could still breathe in this mysterious darkness.

As Davkaleon looked upward, he beheld the monstrous beings closing in on him. Though initially resembling sharks, they swiftly sprouted wings, revealing themselves as chimeras of terror. These creatures far surpassed sharks in ferocity and grotesqueness, boasting giant webbed wings, repulsive gray skin, blood-red eyes, and predatory toothed beaks. Yet amidst their monstrous features, there lingered a disturbingly *human* quality. Counting the currents as he descended, Davkaleon recognized that if this waterfall mirrored the one in Daeya, there was only one means of escape.

Above, looming gray shadows with massive wings could be discerned. Suddenly, a powerful jet from the side struck Davkaleon, sending him spinning like a leaf in the wind. Reacting swiftly, he propelled himself upward on the jet's force, only to be spun around again by another blast from the opposite direction. Undeterred, Davkaleon repeated the process, using each jet's force to propel himself downward once more.

"Seven, eight," Davkaleon counted to himself, clinging to hope amidst the chaos. Another jet slammed into him, sending Davkaleon spinning once more. This time, instead of attempting to counter it, he flattened himself against the force of the jet, allowing it to twist him in an unseen spiral. As the spiral drew nearer to the bottom, its movements became more erratic, resisting release. At the brink of the descent, the spiral thrashed wildly, reluctant to relinquish its hold.

On one side, the waterfall cascaded onto the bottom, transforming into a rushing river that flowed along the ocean floor. On the other side, a narrow streamlet veered away. The spiral's pace slowed marginally, though Davkaleon still found himself caught in its grip, albeit with slightly reduced intensity. Remaining motionless on the jet, Davkaleon observed as the spiral carried him towards the bottom. With each revolution, the spiral propelled him closer until finally, it ejected him into the path of the thin stream. This stream meandered along the ocean floor, diverging from the Tartar River, and leading into the cave beneath the Cliff Rock.

The tunnel led to another cavern, where the water lay tranquil and undisturbed, devoid of even the slightest ripple. Behind him, the gray creatures pursued relentlessly yet now bereft of their wings. Instead, they resembled skeletal monsters, their grotesque, gray, wrinkled skin stretched taut over their bones and skulls.

Despite his initial alarm, Davkaleon charged towards

the creatures. To his astonishment, they paid him no heed, fleeing in the opposite direction. Near one of the walls, a set of stairs ascended upwards, drawing the attention of the Difeserants.

"They've undergone four transformations already," Davkaleon realized. "Their strength must be depleted by now. It's unlikely they fell into the well, prompting their first transformation into winged beings. Sharks marked their second form, followed by monsters with webbed wings as the third, and now these gray skeletons as the fourth. Yet, despite these changes, these Difeserants seem lacking in intelligence. Why undergo such drastic transformations at every turn? Couldn't they simply hold their breath?"

Davkaleon seized the two gray creatures from behind and exerted force to pull them away, sending himself tumbling away from the stairs. He stomped on one and tightly gripped the other, drawing a dagger from his pocket. With swift precision, he dispatched the two gray corpses and swiftly turned his attention to the third Difeserant, squeezing its throat until it went limp with a sickening crunch.

Surveying his surroundings for any remaining threats, Davkaleon spotted another Difeserant attempting to flee, emitting a bubbling sound as it darted towards the cave exit. Davkaleon gave chase, but his pursuit was cut short as he observed the creature ascending and transforming into a shark mid-motion. With a resigned wave of his hand, he retreated, acknowledging the need for rest and reflection.

His best course of action now was to ascend Cliff Rock and ascertain whether it and the Tartar below mirrored their counterparts in Daeya, and whether the surrounding landscape also aligned. Once done, he resolved to return to the Temple and resume his search for the Clock of the Mages.

Davkaleon surveyed the scattered Difeserants, knowing they wouldn't pose a threat for at least the next hour and a half. Initially, they would remain inert, resembling lifeless mummies. Even if one were to stir, it would be in a feeble state, weakened by the recent transformations. They required time to recuperate.

After a brief rest, Davkaleon set his sights on the exit, embarking on his ascent towards the Rock. Scaling the cliff, he took in his surroundings. While the Rock bore a resemblance to its counterpart in Daeya, the similarities ended there. Attl's Cliff Rock sat amidst the open ocean near the outer rampart, encircled by a broad expanse of water. A channel cleaved through the outer shaft, spanned by a couple of bridges.

Upon reaching the outer shaft, Davkaleon leaped down and began swimming towards it. However, his progress was interrupted by the sight of a flock of birds approaching. Davkaleon's senses tingled at the sheer size of the avian creatures, and his apprehension proved warranted. As they closed in on him, their beaks elongated in preparation for an attack. Reacting swiftly, Davkaleon dove into the depths, with the birds in pursuit, transforming into sharks mid-flight.

"Once more, the Difeserants. Oh, I shouldn't have let

that creature out of the cave. It managed to escape—and now, here we go—it's alerted the others," Davkaleon thought bitterly.

The sharks surrounded him, opening their terrible mouths. Davkaleon pressed the ring and began to climb up. The sharks attempted to attack his doppelganger, puzzled as to why they couldn't swallow the fugitive. Davkaleon surfaced and swam to the earthen rampart. Once again, he found himself being pursued by a flock of birds. He had managed to deceive his pursuers with the ring so far, but he could feel fatigue setting in. Davkaleon jumped into the canal and spotted the sharks once more. They weren't very fast this time, but Davkaleon himself was growing weary.

Having ascended the rampart, Davkaleon made his way towards the bridge, followed reluctantly by a flock of birds. With a press of the ring, Davkaleon conjured the illusion of diving into the water. Standing on the bridge, he watched with satisfaction as the creatures, half-birds, and half-sharks, slowly descended into the depths. Leaning against the railing, Davkaleon rested, relishing the touch of the fresh sea breeze on his face. He already felt secure, his gaze drifting towards the distant temple as he estimated the time it would take to reach it.

"Here he is!" Davkaleon heard, turning his head.

A towering black figure, surrounded by slightly smaller companions, scrutinized him closely.

"Are you certain it's him?" inquired the Chief Difeserant.

"Absolutely, Your Excellency. I saw him both in Bible-at-Attl and in the cave under Cliff Rock."

"Again, the Difeserants. This time with their Main One. And how did I manage to let that creature out of the cave?" Davkaleon thought bitterly, preparing to leap off the bridge. However, before he could act, the Main One intercepted him, extending a significantly elongated limb to grab Davkaleon. The other Difeserants closed in from all directions.

"How did you infiltrate Bible-at-Attle?" demanded the Chief menacingly.

As Davkaleon considered whether to respond or to resort to using a weapon and attempting an escape with the ring's aid, one of the attackers growled, "Answer, or I'll swallow you!"

"I'll swallow you myself," the Chief Invisible declared indignantly. "Do you have any idea how he infiltrated Bible-at-Attl? And where did he acquire such precise knowledge about the currents of Tartar? Or perhaps you can enlighten me as to who sent him and what he was seeking in Bible-at-Attl? No answers? Then restrain your hunger."

Another Difeserant added, "Your Headship, I recognize him as well. I spotted him in the Temple. Remember, I reported seeing Varakush in the Temple."

"Ah, so you're also a Varakush. And you traveled from the Temple to Bible-at-Attl. We will have an extensive conversation, and you will not only tell me but also demonstrate. Take him to the Temple. Quickly!" ordered the Chief.

A flock of birds scooped up Davkaleon, carrying him towards the Temple. Observing their trajectory, Davkaleon dismissed the idea of using his weapon and diving into the water. What purpose would it serve? He could always resort to those options later. For now, the flock was leading him in the right direction. They had already reached the inner ring of Attl when a cry pierced the air: "The Highest Priest! The Highest Priest of Attl is returning!"

Davkaleon looked up, spotting the figure of a man descending slowly amidst the clouds. As he reached the ground, the crowd erupted into cheers.

"Get down!" ordered the Chief.

The flock swiftly transformed into somber black figures of the Invisible upon landing. However, amidst the spectacle of the Highest Priest's descent from the heavens, nobody paid them any heed, for all eyes were fixed on the revered figure.

"Ensure he doesn't escape," the Chief ordered, motioning towards Davkaleon.

The Highest Priest had descended near enough to the crowd, and the joyful cries of the Attlids filled the air when a thunderous voice resounded from above: "How dare you, you worthless son of a slave, claim to be the Highest Priest of the great Attl? For such audacity, you shall be struck by lightning!"

Thunder rumbled and bright flashes lit up the sky, causing the Attlids to recoil in fear.

"Despicable Varakush! How dare you speak to the Highest Priest, chosen by the gods themselves?"

The Attlids stood frozen, uncertain of what to do. The Highest Priest of Attl drew nearer, a silvery glow emanating from him. Upon landing, he extended his hand towards Davkaleon and the Invisibles, declaring, "You shall be annihilated on the spot!"

Davkaleon pondered over whom the pronouncement referred to. Was it directed at him, or the Invisible Ones?

The Chief Invisible swiftly intervened, urging Davkaleon forward as he addressed the Highest Priest.

"Oh, greatest of the great Highest Priests of Attl, your devoted Invisibles have apprehended the vile Varakush. We've been tracking him since Bible-at-Attl, where he infiltrated to pilfer the divine manuscripts. We've brought him here, awaiting a just punishment."

"Make way," commanded the Highest Priest.

The crowd obediently shifted back.

With a wave of his hand, the Highest Priest conjured a bonfire on the cleared space.

"Release him," ordered the priest, pointing at Davkaleon.

The Invisibles withdrew.

"Into the fire!" commanded the Priest.

Davkaleon felt an irresistible force propelling him towards the flames. Despite pressing the ring, the unknown force persisted. He took hesitant steps towards the fire, his doppelganger already engulfed in flames. Desperately trying to halt his advance, Davkaleon found himself unable to resist. He neared the blazing inferno, feeling the intense heat, yet compelled to move forward by an unseen power pushing him from behind. With a sigh of relief, he managed to sidestep the flames. However, something or someone continued to urge him forward. As he distanced himself from the fire, he glanced back to see his doppelganger consumed by the blaze.

"Who is guiding me? Is it the Chief Invisible? This isn't good. It means he's aware of the ring." Forced to traverse lengthy corridors, descend into a dungeon, navigate its depths, then emerge and traverse deserted passageways once more, Davkaleon eventually arrived at a small room around a bend. Upon entering, the door vanished behind him, leaving him in a windowless, doorless chamber. Moments later, a chair materialized in the room.

"Not bad," Davkaleon thought, sinking into the chair. "It would be even better with some water." To his surprise, a small table appeared, bearing a decanter filled with clear liquid. "But this is odd! Who could anticipate my needs so precisely?" Davkaleon pondered. "Dear host, would you be so kind as to provide me with a meal?"

The table grew in size, and snacks appeared on it.

"Thank you," Davkaleon bowed and began to eat. It seemed to Davkaleon that several hours had passed; he even dozed off. Sleeping while sitting on a chair was not very comfortable, but the chair adjusted to fit him, transforming into a comfortable armchair. Davkaleon woke up as someone called his name. Another chair in the room held a young man in his mid-twenties. "So, dear Davkaleon, what brings you to my Attl? And why did you take the divine manuscripts from the sacred Bible-at-Attle?"

"I didn't steal the manuscripts! And how do you know my name?"

"The Highest Priest of Attl is supposed to know who visits the sacred sites of his country."

"So, you're the Tot-tze-Attl? Were you the one whom your supposedly Invisible devotees, with the tacit consent of your priests, were planning to strike with lightning upon your return?"

"Yes, you warned me about this, for which I thank you."

"Did I warn you?" Davkaleon was taken aback.

"Yes, it's true. With your characteristic penchant for deceit, you neglected to mention that you were going to steal the divine manuscripts. In Attl, the penalty for such sacrilege is death."

"So, you've essentially condemned me to the bonfire already. I don't know about Attl, but elsewhere, it's not permissible to execute someone twice for the same offense," Davkaleon objected.

"I sentenced Varakush to the bonfire. He had taken to committing various obscenities and terrorizing the Attlids. As for you, firstly, hand over the manuscripts you stole from the Bible-at-Attl."

"I had no intention of stealing the manuscript, but when I had to flee into Tartar because of your Invisibles, I wasn't inclined to return it," Davkaleon said, retrieving the manuscript of the jeweler Piromis from his pocket.

"And the others?" Tot-tze-Attl asked.

"What others?"

"The ones you stole from Bible-at-Attl, of course. My Invisible Ones claimed that you stuffed a dozen, if not more, into your pockets."

"Oh, that's who you trust? Invisible beings? Do you know that your Invisibles are Difeserants? Have you ever seen their muzzles?"

"What do their faces have to do with anything? And who are the Difeserants? Regardless, that's not the matter at hand. For now, I want those stolen manuscripts returned."

Davkaleon felt his hand instinctively emptying its contents from his numerous pockets. Despite his efforts to restrain it on the table, his hand seemed to have a will of its own. Not that Davkaleon had anything to conceal, but it was disconcerting when his own hand refused to obey him.

"You seem to have quite the arsenal," grinned Tot-tze-Attl, observing Davkaleon withdraw knives, daggers, swords, and other far-from-peaceful implements. Next came the emeralds from the jeweler Piromis. "So, you've also taken the emeralds as souvenirs? Well, well, the very honorable Davkaleon. And how did you pay for them? Did you genuinely purchase them from the jeweler's shop?"

"Imagine, I paid honorably and conscientiously," Davkaleon retorted indignantly. "Step into Piromis's shop, open the box of emeralds, and you'll find the gold coins I left behind. They're not Attl's coins, but Daeya's currency; such coins aren't found in your Attl. And regarding the manuscript *theft*, all I intended was to jot down the names of the artifacts Piromis created during his time in the mage's dwelling. Why persist in accusing me of theft?" Davkaleon laid a piece of leather on the table with the list of the jeweler's creations that he had begun.

"Because I've been observing your maneuvers for nearly three years. You're smart, but if resorting to deceit serves your purpose, you won't hesitate for a moment."

"How could you have observed me for three years? This is the first time I've laid eyes on you," Davkaleon exclaimed in surprise.

"Apparently, for you, our meeting, which I'm referring to, hasn't occurred yet. What is this list, and how did you come by it?"

Davkaleon explained. Tot-tze-Attl was unaware of the

jeweler Piromis's adventures in the mage's dwelling or his manuscripts, so for the next half-hour, he listened intently to Davkaleon's account. "So, the first three manuscripts made their way to you in Daeya," remarked Tot-tze-Attl, examining the manuscript from Bible-at-Attl with interest. "And you located this manuscript by its number?" Davkaleon nodded. "What were the numbers of the other two manuscripts?"

Davkaleon provided the numbers 826, 5072, 6097. However, he omitted any mention of the numbers 512, 4913, 5832 from the note found in the Pillantelli cave.

"You can conclude your list of Piromis's products for now, and I'll talk to the Chief Invisible. Also, make sure to transcribe the list twice. I'll keep one copy for myself."

The Highest Priest of Attl touched the wall, and a passage materialized, disappearing as soon as Tot-tze-Attl exited the room. He returned swiftly with unexpected news — the manuscripts bearing the indicated numbers had vanished from the Bible-at-Attl.

"How could they just vanish like that?" Davkaleon exclaimed. "They were there. I saw them!"

"The Invisibles safeguard the manuscripts in Bible-at-Attl. They likely monitored you and discovered that the manuscripts you seek mention the Stone of Destiny, one of Attl's most renowned legends. It's unclear why they've taken them. But let's set aside the matter of the manuscripts for now. How did you manage to enter Attl?"

"Using a Mage's Clock. And with the same Clock, I intend to return. Where is the Clock located in your Temple?"

"Is there a Mage's Clock in this Temple?" Tot-tze-Attl expressed surprise.

"You didn't know? As the Highest Priest of Attl, you're expected to be knowledgeable about all aspects of your Temple."

"I've only recently assumed the role of Highest Priest. Furthermore, I don't believe the Mage's Clock is intended for use by priests. Priests are meant to remain in Attl, not travel between countries and cities. The Clock is more suited for mages. After all, you yourself referred to it as the Mages' Clock. Do you have any recollection of its location? Any distinctive features of signs, doors, corridors? No? That's unfortunate. Well then, let's take a stroll. It's likely the Clock is situated within the abode of the Temple's mages."

Davkaleon was about to mention seeing the Chief Invisible using some kind of amulet to reveal an invisible door in the wall, but Tot-tze-Attl seemed already well acquainted with such Temple features. The Highest Priest moved leisurely through the labyrinthine corridors, his hand adorned with a hefty ring, tracing along the wall. Davkaleon observed with keen interest, anticipating what would unfold. A passage materialized within the flawlessly smooth wall, sealing shut as Tot-tze-Attl and Davkaleon crossed its threshold. Though no clock was immediately visible, after employing the ring's magic several times, Tot-tze-Attl and Davkaleon eventually arrived in a room containing the Clock.

"Perhaps you should mark the wall discreetly for easy access next time," Davkaleon proposed. "Better yet, leave a trail of marks along our path."

"It's futile. We're in the mages' abode within the Temple. Things change swiftly here. Just because the entrance was here a moment ago doesn't guarantee it'll remain in the same spot the next. And it won't."

"How do you navigate through this place?" Davkaleon inquired, astonished.

"With the aid of the Highest Priest's ring," Tot-tze-Attl responded.

"And if I possessed such a ring, could I also reveal invisible doors?" Davkaleon sought clarification, hastening to add, "I solemnly swear on my honor that I have no intention of tampering with your ring. I simply seek to understand the workings of magic."

Whether Tot-tze-Attl believed Davkaleon's assurances remained unclear, but he proceeded to address Davkaleon's inquiry.

"Firstly, you wouldn't be able to obtain my ring. You must have noticed by now that I can compel you to do as I wish, as evidenced when I dispatched your doppelganger into the fire and guided you into the Temple. Secondly, even if I were to give you the Highest Priest's ring, it would be of no use to you. To wield its power, you'd need to undergo all the requisite initiations, and my blood would need to course through your veins, as the ring was crafted specifically for me in accordance with sacred Attl's rituals." As they approached the Clock, Davkaleon noticed the familiar depiction of 2519 within a circle.

"I won't require that just yet," Davkaleon mused. "For now, I need to reach Heather, so I must locate the panel she mentioned." Davkaleon scrutinized the desired symbol and, manipulating the panel, arranged the arrows as Heather had instructed.

Chapter 20. Astera

Davkaleon found himself standing near the fountain at the entrance to the temple and proceeded inside.

A voice boomed from somewhere above. "What are you doing here?!" Davkaleon could have sworn it was the voice of the temple in the rock.

"I discovered how to enter Twierks, so I completed your assignment," Davkaleon explained.

"The trickster! You arrived here using the Mages' Clock, yet the task was entirely different."

"Dear Lord of the Twierks! Cheating is not a crime, but rather *resourcefulness*. I managed the Clock, and I'll manage your assignment. I am a capable student," Davkaleon responded, clearly concerned about the temple's disapproval.

"Ah, cheating is not a crime, but resourcefulness? Swindler!"

"The Honorable Lord of the Twierks," Davkaleon began, but the lord cut him off.

"Don't flatter me! What brings you here?"

"I've come to seek an audience with Priestess Mistletoe," Davkaleon explained.

"And why do you seek Mistletoe?"

Before Davkaleon could respond, he found that he didn't have to. He wasn't sure how the invisible interlocutor would react to his request, but Mistletoe herself entered the temple.

"Dear Priestess Mistletoe," Davkaleon addressed her. "You may know me by the name of Abal-Dural. May I have a moment of your time?"

The priestess looked at Davkaleon with surprise. "So, you do exist," she sneered. "Very well, follow me."

In Mistletoe's office now, Davkaleon noticed the Mage's Clock on display. After presenting lavish gifts on Mistletoe's table, Davkaleon inquired about Heather.

"Heather has been sent to study at the high priestess school of ISIDA," Mistletoe replied, glancing indifferently at the offerings.

"When did this happen?" Davkaleon queried.

"Just recently," Mistletoe responded.

"Where is this school located?" Davkaleon asked, disappointment evident in his voice.

"I cannot disclose that information," Mistletoe stated firmly.

"Heather is in need of protection, she's being pursued by the Difeserants."

"And you provide this protection?" Mistletoe laughed incredulously. This young man was certainly confident!

"Absolutely! If I marry Heather, not a single hair on her head will be harmed—" Davkaleon was abruptly interrupted. An unseen force descended upon him, threatening to toss him out like a wisp of fluff. Reacting swiftly, Davkaleon seized the Mage's Clock. With a whirl, he found himself in an unfamiliar room. Scanning his surroundings, he noticed the dimly lit space lacked any visible exits, though he couldn't be sure in the dimness.

"What brings you here?" Davkaleon heard a voice and turned to find a man seated at the table, his features obscured by a broad-brimmed hat.

"I seek entry to the high priestess school of ISIDA,"

Davkaleon replied.

"And why is that?" the man queried.

"My fiancée is a student there," Davkaleon explained.

"Your fiancée? Since when do ISIDA students enter into marriage without the blessing of the goddess?" The obscure figure grinned.

"She's in danger and requires protection," Davkaleon responded, sidestepping the stranger's inquiry.

With a snap of his fingers, the stranger summoned a massive, hairy spider into the room. Without hesitation, Davkaleon swiftly dispatched it with his sword. However, both halves dissolved into a swirling black mist, quickly filling the room, and causing Davkaleon to struggle for breath.

"What kind of protector are you? You seem to need protecting yourself," the stranger laughed.

"What are your terms for aiding me in reaching her?" Davkaleon asked, feeling the suffocating pressure of the mist.

"This is a matter for negotiation," the stranger in the hat replied coolly. As suddenly as it appeared, the black fog dissipated. "Well then," the stranger continued, "let's see what you're capable of. Your priests have recently instigated conflict with the priestesses of Llill. My friend Astera remains in their custody, accused of dark sorcery. Set her free, and then we can discuss Heather."

"I'll ensure her release," Davkaleon agreed with relief. "How can I reach you afterwards?"

"Astera will find me when the time is right," the stranger replied cryptically.

A familiar whirlwind enveloped Davkaleon, transporting him to the grove near Assa. From there, it was a short journey to Carducci's shop, which Davkaleon visited without delay. "Here's a list of magical artifacts crafted by the jeweler Piromis and the mage," Davkaleon explained, displaying the list.

"Excellent," the proprietor of the magic shop said. "Were you able to acquire anything from this list?"

"Hold on a moment," Davkaleon said, tempering his enthusiasm. "The manuscripts are housed in the Attl library, numbering in the millions. Without knowing the approximate number, locating the Piromis manuscript would be like finding a needle in a haystack. I managed to identify three of the jeweler's manuscripts with known numbers and confirmed their authenticity compared to those in Daeya. The first two were identical, while the third was longer, detailing additional artifacts crafted by Piromis. Before my next visit to Attl, I'll need to ascertain the manuscript numbers."

"Understood. Is there anything else?" Carducci inquired.

"Yes, there's still a Piromis jeweler's shop in Attl, which offers replicas of the Stone of Destiny. I purchased a few as mementos. Here's one for you, as a token of gratitude for facilitating my access to Attl," Davkaleon stated, retrieving an emerald from his pocket.

"An exquisite emerald," remarked the shopkeeper, examining the stone. "When do you plan to return to Attl?"

"As soon as I obtain the manuscript numbers," Davkaleon replied.

"A thousand sickles," suggested Davkaleon.

"Ten thousand," one of the men replied.

"Two thousand," Davkaleon doubled his offer.

"Ten!" Another snapped.

"Three?"

"Ten!!!"

Bargaining between Davkaleon and the priests of the temple (where Astera was kept) continued. "Okay, ten it is," Davkaleon waved his hand, realizing that there would be no discount. He laid out the money.

A few minutes later, Astera appeared in the room. Concealed beneath an oversized cape, she resembled a black cocoon, wrapped from head to toe. If there was anything attractive hidden under this cape, it would be difficult to discern.

"I need money, candles, a crystal ball, a ritual dagger, a bowl, a mirror, and candlesticks," Astera said as soon as they left the temple.

With money, candles, and candlesticks covered, Davkaleon could easily find a mirror and a bowl. "Where can I get a crystal ball and a ritual dagger?"

"How would I know where to find a crystal ball and a ritual dagger in this God-forsaken place of Daeya?" Astera shrugged.

Sighing, Davkaleon headed to the magic shop. When he asked about the ritual dagger, the owner asked, "Which one do you prefer? Bolin? Jag? Six? Al-Damm?"

Davkaleon's expression went blank. The owner of the magic shop realized that without guiding questions, he would inevitably lose a customer. "What kind of ritual do you intend to perform?"

"What? Do ritual daggers need to be different for various rituals?" Davkaleon asked. As he glanced at the shopkeeper, he realized his question sounded foolish. Instead, he said, "I think I'll take them all. I might need to perform another ritual in the dead of night, and I can't come running to you."

"Ah, blessed words! Perform your rituals whenever, wherever, and however you wish," the shopkeeper smiled warmly.

Upon hearing the total amount, Davkaleon worried over money. Fortunately, he had enough, but he had to ensure to buy a small crystal ball as well.

"Why do I have to wait so long? Where's my lunch?" Astera exclaimed as soon as Davkaleon appeared at the threshold.

"I gave you money. Why didn't you buy whatever lunch you wanted?" Davkaleon objected.

"What? So, I would be distracted by such nonsense?" Astera retorted, clearly indignant.

Silently cursing to himself, Davkaleon went to fetch lunch for Astera.

"As soon as Davkaleon placed the meal in front of her, she cried, "Steak?! What are you doing?! It's bad for my stomach! I need a tender cutlet."

Davkaleon had already opened his mouth to voice his thoughts about tender cutlets, but he remembered in time that Astera was his only lead to Heather. Cursing the witchiest witch he had ever met, Davkaleon begrudgingly went to find a cutlet.

The second lunch fared no better. "Fried?! Cooked in vile animal fat? What are you thinking! I won't eat such filth. I need a steamed cutlet!"

Davkaleon imagined with horror the prospect of going to the *Mug and Sword*, encountering half of his schoolmates, and asking the waiter to prepare a steamed cutlet. They'd ridicule him!

"Hydragon!" Davkaleon called out to his three-headed pet, but it was nowhere to be found.

"Hydragon, I'm offering you a delicious meal!" Unfortunately, Hydragon didn't appear.

"Hydragon, I've been feeding you for a whole week." No answer.

"Two!" Three of Hydragon's heads appeared at the door.

Davkaleon nodded. *Two it is. Better than becoming the subject of schoolyard tales about steamed cutlets.*

"Don't you dare imply this is for me," Davkaleon warned Hydragon.

He fared no better when he presented the daggers.

"Tin? Copper? Iron? What are you thinking?! Those are men's daggers! I need a silver one. Silver daggers possess a gentle feminine energy. During rituals, it flows like water," Astera remarked without even glancing at the steamed cutlet Davkaleon had brought.

"Silver? Could you not have mentioned that earlier?" Davkaleon retorted indignantly.

"How was I supposed to know you were so clueless? You were sent for me by the Great Mage himself. How could you even catch his eye if you're so ignorant? When he asks for my opinion about you—"

"Alright, alright. You'll have your silver dagger," Davkaleon quickly gave in to Astera's demands.

"I need a ritual dagger," Astera demanded the next day.

"I bought one for you," Davkaleon protested.

"You bought me a dagger with a black handle, but I need one with a white handle. And also one with a red handle. Each ritual requires its own dagger."

The requests for different daggers, candlesticks, and mirrors came with enviable consistency.

"Give me a complete list of what you need at once, and don't bombard me every day," Davkaleon insisted.

"Well, am I supposed to remember all the rituals?"

Davkaleon turned green but managed to compose himself.

"This mirror isn't reflective enough," Astera complained the next day.

"What?!"

"The ritual isn't working," Astera lamented, spreading her hands. "The mirror doesn't mirror, the ritual doesn't ritual."

"Fine, I'll bring you the one hundred and first mirror right now!" Davkaleon fumed, storming toward the door.

"You should send someone else so you and I can sit and talk. Otherwise, I'm bored," remarked Astera.

"Let's go choose a mirror together, and you can select the one you want," Davkaleon suggested, realizing he couldn't endure more than five minutes alone with Astera.

Davkaleon attempted to divert communication with Astera to Hydragon. Ha! Hydragon had vanished, even going hunting (an activity he had never engaged in before). If it hadn't been for the stranger's promise that Astera would contact him as she saw fit, Davkaleon would have ejected the mage's girlfriend from the temple dungeon on the first day of her release. But how would he find Heather if he did? Davkaleon felt an urgent need to take action before he strangled Astera himself.

"How much are you willing to be tethered to your mage?" he asked bluntly.

"You're not ready yet," Astera replied cryptically.

*****

Observing the unfolding events, Adamant and Ecktoral burst into laughter.

"Where did you find this Astera?" Adamant asked, watching Davkaleon kick the stone wall in frustration after yet another outlandish claim from the witch.

"It's Eximi's doing," Ecktoral grinned. "Seems he should have pursued acting rather than becoming a mage. I wanted to see if Davkaleon would take actions for Heather that he wouldn't have taken otherwise. He certainly wouldn't tolerate Astera for a whole month," Ecktoral explained.

"No doubt about that," Adamant agreed. "Let your mage subject him to a rigorous test. Let's see what he's capable of. I know his knowledge is next to nothing now. I'm curious to see if he's even capable of learning. And don't forget to arrange some of his favorite competitions for him to miss. Whether it's with cards or dragons. Let's see what he would do."

Davkaleon lamented to his brother Elfid about Astera and his miserable existence. "Can you imagine? I purchased that cursed witch from the priests, and it ended up costing me much more than I anticipated. But money aside, instead of showing gratitude for being spared from the stake, that cursed witch commands me. Do this, fetch that. I've even offered her money, but she refuses to accept it! I feel like I want to throttle her ten times a day, and that's that. If you don't advise me on what to offer her so she'll arrange for me to meet her sorcerer, I'm at my wit's end."

"A potion from the Llill witches might be of help. It could make Astera more compliant. Just be cautious with the dosage; if you overdo it, she might enjoy it and decide to stay with you indefinitely. Add only one drop to her food, and after a few days, broach the topic of meeting a mage," Elfid suggested.

Davkaleon followed the advice diligently. He painstakingly added one drop at a time. Unfortunately, this had no effect on Astera. Davkaleon doubled the dose, but still, Astera's demeanor remained unchanged. Frustrated, he angrily poured half a bottle into her food. Astera turned green, then blue.

"What did you add here, you jerk?" The witch rose to the ceiling. She calmed down quickly enough. Extending a glass, Astera demanded, "Pour more."

The potion had a peculiar effect on Astera. She declared, "I'm tired of you, I'm leaving."

"And what about my meeting with the mage?"

Davkaleon was taken aback.

"Get ready, you have two minutes. Take all my daggers, crystal balls, and everything else. Be careful with the mirrors. If you scratch one, you won't create a mirrored corridor, and without a corridor, you won't find the mage. And if you break the mirror, it's a major disaster."

"Now?! Can't we do it tomorrow? I have a competition right now. Dragon flights!" Davkaleon was seriously horrified at the thought of missing the competition.

"What else," Astera chuckled, "Why should I linger in this poverty until tomorrow? I've already invested so much time in you!"

"You? Invested in me? Did I ask you to do that? And besides, in poverty? This is the best quarter in Daeya!" Davkaleon clenched his teeth. After all, Astera was finally relenting, even appearing to intend to accompany him to the mage. What more could he want? It was just a shame to miss the competition. His faithful dragon, Aleurh, might have scolded him for such a ploy. Seizing the moment, he contacted Elfid — there must be some benefit from the Adoleeseet's transmitter, a gift from Chapa. The transmitter functioned flawlessly.

"Elfid, Astera is taking me to a mage. Inform Aleurh that I will miss the competition," he requested of his brother.

"Who are you talking to in there?" Astera poked her nose into the room.

"No one. I'm just talking to myself."

"You owe me twenty thousand sickles!" Astera demanded.

"What???"

"What did you expect? That I perform rituals for free? And bear in mind, if you don't have the money, I won't wait for you. Where I'm headed, beggars are not welcome. I've devoted an entire month to you! And you haven't even bought me a single golden dagger!"

"Okay, okay. I'll find the money," Davkaleon said, meticulously searching his wallet and all his numerous pockets. Not entirely convinced that he was finally getting rid of Astera, Davkaleon laid out everything he had gathered.

Astera protested, meticulously counting the money. "It's five sickles short."

"I spent it on your lunch," Davkaleon growled.

"A miser," Astera sneered.

Davkaleon swiftly packed daggers, crystal balls, and small mirrors into bags. However, dealing with the large mirrors proved more challenging. There were four of them, and Davkaleon didn't have a bag large enough to contain them.

"Be careful not to break them. Otherwise, forget about meeting the mage," Astera warned.

They left the house and headed towards the grove near Assa.

"Wait a moment, I'll fetch Aleurh, my dragon," Davkaleon offered. "He can take us anywhere you want in no time."

"I don't need your Aleurh," Astera snapped. "He'll start poking his nose into everything – where, what, and why. I don't like it. Let's take the mail dragon one way. You can walk back...you won't fall apart."

Davkaleon clenched his teeth tightly, refraining from expressing his true feelings about Astera and her proposal. Having settled with Astera, Davkaleon found himself without any money left. He offered to provide a receipt, but the dragon declined.

"I know you," the dragon said, "your life is unpredictable. Who's to say whether you'll live to see tomorrow? I could end up without payment."

Searching through his pockets, Davkaleon retrieved a pair of precious stones. (He always kept something valuable in case coins weren't sufficient, like for gambling.)

"Fine, let's have them," the dragon relented.

"To the dragon grove," Astera commanded.

The dragon grove held memories of Davkaleon's duel with Krasius Pompeus a few years ago. It was also known for its association with black magic. As the mail dragon landed, Davkaleon unloaded the bags and mirrors.

Once the dragon had flown away, Astera instructed them to descend.

"Where do we descend?" Davkaleon scanned the surroundings. Right behind him was a bottomless black abyss. A suspended staircase led downward. It was quite inconvenient to navigate while juggling a couple of large bags and carrying four huge mirrors. Davkaleon consoled himself with the thought that it could have been worse if the cursed witch had insisted on being carried too. "I'm exhausted," Astera complained, "carry me."

"How? I only have two hands."

"That's enough," miraculously, Astera found herself in his arms. Davkaleon felt as though the slightest movement could send them tumbling down with the witch, mirrors, and bags.

"You know, it just occurred to me that I'd miss you if you fell," Astera remarked. "We should widen the stairs." Instantly, the staircase transformed into a comfortable, spacious descent with a sturdy handrail. Davkaleon's fear of falling dissipated. However, the challenge of carrying bags, mirrors, *and* Astera remained.

"Let me lower the mirrors and bags first, then I'll come back for you," Davkaleon suggested.

"Don't. I've decided I'm content with you as well. Let's head back. Time to go home."

"Oh, gods! Elfid was right about the potion," Davkaleon thought. "I accidentally gave her the entire potion. What do I do now?"

"Davkaleon-Shka," Astera purred, "forget about that mage. Let's hurry back to your house."

Davkaleon grew deeply concerned by this sudden change of heart. "I cannot allow you to stay in my humble abode. It's not fitting for you. We must reach the mage swiftly. He'll conjure a palace of royal luxury for you."

"Do you truly believe I need a mage for that? I'll do as I please," Astera shrugged. "Witness."

The stairs descended on their own accord. At the bottom of the abyss lay gardens and flower beds. Birds sang melodious tunes in the trees, while goldfish frolicked in the lake. Astera nodded, and a marble palace materialized before Davkaleon's eyes. Dwarves emerged from the palace, bowing deeply to Davkaleon as they carried the bags and mirrors inside. A carpet with two armchairs glided out of the doorway and unfurled at Davkaleon's feet.

"Have a seat," the witch suggested. "Behold your new domain."

Davkaleon panicked. He knew how to handle Astera's witchery, but he was at a loss against her sudden affection.

"It's quite solitary here. I'm accustomed to my own home," Davkaleon remarked.

"What would you have me do—relocate your street here or erect a palace with a garden on your street?" Astera asked.

Davkaleon realized that feeble excuses wouldn't suffice. Bracing for conflict, he informed Astera that he was already engaged.

"What?!" Astera soared to the skies.

If Davkaleon thought he was able to imagine the subsequent troubles, then he was very wrong. Astera stamped her feet, screamed, and brought down the newly created palace. The gardens with flowers and birds disappeared, the lake with goldfish vanished. Instead of a lake, a swamp with croaking frogs appeared. Instead of singing birds, toothy lizards with webbed wings flew in the sky. But that was just the beginning. Davkaleon had to fully experience the fury of an angry witch.

"Who is she? Who is your fiancée?" Astera moved closer.

Davkaleon took a step back.

"Show her!" Astera demanded.

"I don't have her portrait," Davkaleon tried to dodge.

"I'll get her portrait myself," Astera snapped.

Davkaleon felt that an unknown force was squeezing his head like a red-hot hoop. The next moment, he saw a foggy image of Heather in the air. The fog was thickening, and after a minute Heather was looking around in surprise. Davkaleon rushed to the girl and felt that he could not take a single step. He, or rather his boots, stuck to the viscous sticky goo flowing out of the swamp. The sticky goo was creeping up on Heather. The girl has not seen this yet. Continuing to look around, the girl saw Davkaleon.

"Davkaleon," she rejoiced, and, taking a step, got bogged down in the mud.

Astera held out her hand in Heather's direction. Thousands of sparks sparkled around the girl's bracelets. Heather looked at her bracelets in surprise.

"What? Is your fiancée an apprentice of the priestesses of ISIDA?" Astera screamed. "ISIDA's students are forbidden to marry. That's not what they're trained for at school! This is not going to happen! I will destroy it! I'll kill her! I will exterminate her!"

Davkaleon was horrified to see two black-robed figures appear behind Heather. Unseen, they were the Difeserants who stretched out their paws to Heather.

"Heather, don't be afraid," Davkaleon shouted to the girl and, pulling a pair of knives out of his pocket, threw them at the Difeserants.

Heather screamed and looked around. Davkaleon's knives cut off one paw from each monster.

"Don't move," Davkaleon shouted again and threw the second pair of knives. For just a moment, each of the Difeserants was without a pair of paws, but new limbs were already growing in their place. Davkaleon had many knives and daggers, but he knew only fire could cope with the Difeserants. Davkaleon took a flint from his pocket. Not finding anything more suitable, he tore off his shirt sleeve without hesitation, tore it in half and, tying it to a pair of knives, set it on fire. "Heather, get down," he shouted as he threw flaming knives at the Difeserants.

Davkaleon had a couple more knives in his pockets. He pulled one out and yanked the boots open from the bottom up. Now he could get out of them. However, he was not sure if he would be able to jump out and jump to the place without sticky goo. And Astera held out her hand towards Heather again. The next Difeserants were about to appear.

The toothy lizards were still flying in the sky. They looked very predatory at possible prey. They did not like the endless throwing of knives by Davkaleon, but they did not fly away, they waited for the knives to run out. One of the lizards decided not to mess with Davkaleon and went to Heather. Davkaleon threw a knife at his throat, and the beast fell to the ground. Another lizard, circling over Heather, prepared to attack.

Davkaleon jerked out the adamantine sword. It's a good thing he bought it at Twierks Tavern. True, he paid a crazy amount for it, but no other sword could have withstood what Davkaleon wanted to do. Leaving the remains of his boots in the sticky muck, Davkaleon jumped. Holding the sword down, he pushed off from it and, after flying a couple more meters, landed in a dry place.

"It won't work," Astera screamed, and two more Difeserants appeared next to Heather, and Davkaleon was back in the sticky muck.

Pulling out the last knife, Davkaleon swung it to launch it at the witch. At the last moment, he grabbed the knife with his other hand. If he kills Astera, how will he get to the mage? True, Heather is with him now, but she was with him during the Thanksgiving holiday, and the silver arrow took her away from him. Davkaleon did not even notice that, grabbing the blade of the knife, he cut himself badly.

Blood dripped onto the ground. The blood hissed as it mixed with the sticky goo. The Difeserants, flying lizards and croaking frogs have disappeared. Along with them, the swamp, the sticky goo, and the ruins of the castle disappeared. Heather is missing too. There was no deep abyss. Davkaleon was in the grove. His daggers were scattered on the ground. There were slashed boots and the remains of a torn shirt sleeve lying next to him. An adamantine sword was stuck in the ground. Not far from Davkaleon there were two large bags with ritual daggers and a hundred small mirrors. There were large mirrors next to the bag. They were all intact, but Astera was gone.

"Oh gods, how am I going to find a mage now?" Davkaleon was horrified. Davkaleon remembered that Astera had said something about a mirrored corridor. However, Davkaleon did not know what it was, so he contacted Elfid.

"Yes, I know what a mirrored corridor is," Elfid replied. "This is a dangerous thing. Why do you need it?"

Davkaleon told him what had happened.

"So, you're in the grove?" Elfid clarified.

"Well, yes. And the mirrors are all with me. But I do not know what to do with them."

"You put one mirror against another; you also put something between them. In the mirrors, there is a reflection of what you put between the mirrors, and then another reflection of the reflection, and so on. In general, a corridor of smaller and smaller mirror reflections is visible," Elfid explained.

"I see. And what about the other mirrors?" Davkaleon asked.

"What others?" Elfid did not understand.

"I have four large mirrors and a hundred small ones here," Davkaleon explained.

"There are a lot of things you can do with mirrors. For a mirrored corridor, you only need two mirrors. What Astera wanted to do with the other mirrors, only she knows. The main thing is not to put yourself between the mirrors. It's dangerous, you may not come back from this corridor, or give all your strength to your mirror doppelganger, or meet someone not from our world," Elfid said.

Astera said that I wouldn't see a mage without a mirrored corridor. Now I'll meet the mage without her," Davkaleon rejoiced.

Elfid tried to convince Davkaleon to abandon the dangerous venture, but did not succeed. After finishing the conversation with his brother, Davkaleon set up two mirrors one against the other and stood between them. In the mirror he was looking into, he saw a corridor of smaller and smaller reflections of himself. The smallest reflection that could still be seen waved at him.

"Did you miss me, my Davkaleon-shka?" The reflection asked in Astera's voice.

Davkaleon recoiled, and Astera smiled happily. Davkaleon removed the mirrors and replaced them with two others. Alas, Astera has not gone anywhere. After trying different options, Davkaleon installed four mirrors. It turned out to be something like a cubicle with mirrored walls. He could still see Astera in the mirrored corridor, but the mage was reflected in the side mirrors.

"My dear Astera-shka told me that she wants to marry you," said the mage. "I decided to bless you."

"No!!!" Davkaleon shouted in horror.

"Why not?" I'll give you a good dowry for my Astera-shka."

A mountain of gold coins appeared next to Davkaleon.

Davkaleon shook his head stubbornly.

"Not enough? I'll give you more." The mountain of gold increased in size. "You aspire to become the commander-in-chief of Daeya's army. I'll support you. Once you achieve that position, I'll allocate more funds for army rearmament. You'll emerge as the premier commander-in-chief in Daeya's history. Tales of your prowess will spread far and wide."

"No, I'll attain the position of commander-in-chief on my own. And I'll secure the funds for army rearmament,"

Davkaleon asserted stubbornly.

"Well, it seems you're quite obstinate, not to mention foolish," the mage retorted, visibly irritated. "You can't even afford a decent pair of boots." The mirror reflected Davkaleon's worn-out footwear.

"You pledged to transport me to Heather once I liberated Astera. I've fulfilled my end. Now, it's time for you to honor your promise," Davkaleon pressed.

"You're quite persistent, aren't you? I never explicitly made that promise, but fine, let's discuss it," the mage conceded begrudgingly.

The next moment, Davkaleon found himself in a dimly lit room devoid of windows or doors. It was the same room where he had first encountered the stranger.

Chapter 21. A Journey to the School of Mixed Time

"Are you certain you wish to proceed?" the stranger queried.

"Absolutely! Why else would I tolerate that Astera witch?! I'm sorry if you happen to fancy her, but she's like a thorn in my side," Davkaleon retorted, his frustration evident.

The stranger's grin widened at the mention of Astera, yet he remained unfazed by Davkaleon's outburst. "No one will permit Heather to vanish from the Priestesses of ISIDA High School, especially over something as trivial as your desire to wed her. That's not the reason she was sent there."

"But she's in danger, and the Difeserants are pursuing her.

"Any decent amulet will shield her from the Difeserants," the stranger dismissed with a wave of his hand. "Once she graduates, she won't fear any monsters; she'll banish them in an instant. However, she'll still face dangers beyond the grasp of an ordinary barbarian like yourself."

"Who are you calling an ordinary barbarian?!" Davkaleon protested, his pride wounded.

"What did you expect? That you're Daeya's greatest intellect?" the stranger retorted.

"I'm not claiming to be Daeya's greatest intellect, but Heather doesn't require that. She isn't drawn to formulas herself," Davkaleon countered.

"Whether or not she's drawn to formulas is inconsequential," the stranger shrugged.

"You mentioned that even after graduation, she'll be in danger. What kind?" Davkaleon inquired.

"Battles with black magicians, encounters with evil *khmers*. One Prann is worth a lot!" the stranger replied cryptically.

The term *khmer* puzzled Davkaleon, so he disregarded it, but he was aware of the threat posed by Prann.

"A confrontation with Prann?! And you plan to leave her alone? Send me to her!" Davkaleon insisted.

"And how do you propose to aid her? You'll only serve as a distraction from her studies. Once she graduates and becomes a Priestess of ISIDA, a mere mortal like yourself will not be part of her path," the stranger countered.

Davkaleon argued vehemently. "How much will you charge me to attend this school? I'll pay for it! Leave the battles with Prann and other horrors to me; don't burden Heather with them. I'm graduating from military school. Combat is a man's duty; don't saddle her with it!"

The stranger tapped their fingers on the table, contemplating Davkaleon's words. "I fail to see much merit in sending you to school. You're nearly 18, and you've lagged behind for quite some time. You're preoccupied with fights, cards, and adventures, not to mention romance with Heather. You've never shown much interest in studying."

"If my studies assist me in facing Prann, I'll devote myself to the formulas and pay whatever is necessary," Davkaleon proposed earnestly.

"It's costly. Daeya lacks such funds. You were taken aback by the price of the Mages' Clock; attending this school is considerably more expensive."

"If you're aware of the Mages' Clock, then you must also know about the enchanted jewelry crafted by the jeweler Piromis. They can cover the expenses of my education. I'll obtain them for you!" Davkaleon declared confidently.

The mage chuckled. "Very well, I'll grant you an opportunity. To locate Piromis's jewelry, you must decipher the note you discovered in the Pillantelli cave. Heather and your brother aided you with the sketches. Only numerical clues remain. You have access to the Depository of Knowledge and limitless time. If hunger strikes, sustenance will materialize. Fatigue will summon a bed as if by magic. The doors of learning are wide open. The only restriction is that the Depository won't provide direct answers about the numbers on the note, but you can access as many books as you need. Whether you spend a day, a month, or a year within its confines is inconsequential. Whenever you depart, it will be as though no time has passed. However, if you exit before uncovering the solution, you'll lose sight of Twierks and Heather forever, and the temple in the rock will be but a distant memory. Proceed! The entrance awaits."

*****

Davkaleon read the definition of a mathematical sequence for the tenth time, genuinely perplexed as to how this definition would help him unravel the mystery of the numbers from the note. The sequence of numbers from the note was ingrained in his memory: 512, 4913, 5832.

Try as he might, Davkaleon couldn't discern any clear pattern in these numbers, nor could he fathom what the next number in the sequence should be. Despite his efforts, the Depository continued to supply him with textbook after textbook.

A couple of weeks had passed in the Depository. Davkaleon received the task of finding the number following 125.

$$8, 27, 64, 125 \ldots$$

As long as the Depository was messing with his head with sequences like squares, he was doing fine, but the numbers in question were clearly not squares.

"Could they be cubes?" Davkaleon thought and looked at the cheat sheet he had made. The cheat sheet contained a lot of information, including a table of cubes. "That's right! Here they all are!" rejoiced Davkaleon.

$2^3 = 8$

$3^3 = 27$

$4^3 = 64$

$5^3 = 125$

"The next one would be 6^3. Now, where is 6^3? How much is it? Oh, here it is: $6^3 = 216$."

Davkaleon gazed at the table. His gaze carelessly slid to the number 512. In the next moment, he jumped up from his seat. In the table, it was clearly stated: $8^3 = 512$. That's the number from the note! So, all the numbers from the note were also cubes?

In his cheat sheet was a table of cubes from 1 to 10. The largest in the table was $10^3 = 1000$. The next numbers in the note were obviously bigger. It's reasonable to do the math to test a hunch like that. It took Davkaleon a long time to do the calculations. Arithmetic was clearly not his strong suit. But after a few hours, Davkaleon looked at the numbers he had obtained, unable to believe his luck.

$8^3 = 512$

$17^3 = 4913$

$18^3 = 5832$

In front of him were the numbers from the note:

512,   4913,   5832

8^3 17^3 18^3

So, it was clear with the numbers indicated in the note. But what will be the next number? What do 8, 17, and 18 have in common?

Many days passed before Davkaleon realized the trick. And once he did, he began to search for the next number. So, there was a clue in front of him. The sum of the digits of each number, cubed, was equal to the number itself.

$512 \rightarrow (5+1+2 = 8)^3 = 8^3 = 512$

$4913 \rightarrow (4+9+1+3 = 17)^3 = 17^3 = 4913$

$5832 \rightarrow (5+8+3+2 = 18)^3 = 18^3 = 5832$

Davkaleon had been calculating the next number for a long time. He even tried to negotiate with the Depository of Knowledge.

"I've figured out the trick to this sequence. Now, only arithmetic is left. If I hire a dozen mathematicians, they'll have it figured out in no time..."

"No, you won't hire any mathematicians," the Depository answered. "You have to do the math yourself. And don't quibble if you want the Great Mage to give you credit for passing the test."

Sighing, Davkaleon began to calculate. Eventually, he got through this one, too.

$$17576 \rightarrow (1+7+5+7+6 = 26)^3 = 26^3 = 17576$$

*****

"I'll send you to the school," the mage said, "but not for romance with Heather, but for studying, so there will be a surprise waiting for you there. And if I don't like something about your behavior, then you will immediately find yourself in the Daeya. And I'll make sure that you never get to Twierks and see Heather. Is that clear?"

Davkaleon nodded.

"You will go to the School of Mixed Times," the mage continued. "If they ask you how you got there, answer that you were sent by an almighty mage, and that you don't know the name of this mage."

Davkaleon agreed.

"Enter this door," the mage nodded towards the opposite wall, "and you will find yourself in a secret cave." Davkaleon turned his head to where the stranger was pointing. He could have sworn that there was no door here a moment ago.

"Say the words 'School of Mixed Times' to yourself," the mage continued, "and there will be an exit in the cave. You will come out of the cave and see a clearing with a stream. There is a path near the stream that will lead you to the hill. Under the hill, you will see a building surrounded by a fence. You'll go inside. This is the School of Mixed Times. At the entrance, you will be asked for documents – here they are," the mage handed over the package and continued, "you need Quantrell Frost. Give him this letter."

At the same moment, Davkaleon found himself holding an envelope and a note with instructions on what to do.

"Enter the building, take the elevator down to the twentieth underground floor, you will find a room with the number -20345. This is the office of Quantrell Frost, extreme analyst of the experimental department of the Institute of Space and Time," Davkaleon read.

"The elevator? An extreme analyst? The Institute of Space and Time? What kind of gibberish is this?" Davkaleon was surprised, but there was no one to ask. The mage disappeared.

Davkaleon did as the mage ordered.

After waiting in the hallway for a few minutes and observing what the others were doing, he figured out the elevator. Once on the right floor, Davkaleon headed for the room with the number -20345. On the way, an inscription on the bulletin board caught his attention.

"The seminar on problems arising from time travel is postponed two weeks ago."

"Well, well," Davkaleon thought and opened the door.

Inside, he saw a group of strangers. Most of them looked like dwarfs, none reaching two meters in height. In the center of the room was a table, at which sat what appeared to be Quantrell Frost. "Greetings..." Davkaleon began, glancing around the audience.

The next moment, he spotted the one who had stolen Heather from him. With a loud cry of "Where is she?" Davkaleon leaped across the room and grabbed the dwarf by the throat.

Epilogue

"If I remember correctly, Eximi is the mage who created Piromis's jewels?" Adamant clarified.

"Well, yes," Ecktoral nodded.

"So, your Davkaleon offered to pay for the studying with artifacts created by the mage himself?" Adamant smiled.

Ecktoral nodded.

"Davkaleon will meet Heather at the school. Do you really expect them to meet each other, say 'hi,' and start studying the equations of quantum physics together? Personally, I think he's gonna try to kidnap her. And if he doesn't do it on the first day, it'll be for one reason only - he'll have to find a place to hide her," Adamant grinned.

"He'd try, but I've planned for that and prepared a trick," Ecktoral smiled.

"Your Davkaleon is a good fighter, but he won't become a brilliant physicist. It would be good if he had a basic understanding of what's going on in Twierks. Let your mage Eximi pick a few talented and adventurous teenagers from somewhere between the 21st and 22nd centuries. Add to their company a few girls who still have the genes from the Llill's combination. We can't rule out our rival friends getting close to Heather too soon."

"Finding them in the 21st and 22nd centuries won't be easy. The Church Inquisition was not in vain," Ecktoral said.

"It's a big planet. You promised your mage Eximi an unprecedented reward. Let him work for it."

TO BE CONTINUED

NOTE FROM THE AUTHOR

If you enjoyed DRAGONS DO NOT WRITE MEMOIRS,
please leave a review online. Even if it is just a sentence or two.
It would be very much appreciated.

Thanks!

Tetyana Butler